BETRAYAL OF THIEVES

C. Greenwood

A BEGINNING

T OSSING IN MY HAMMOCK, I try to ignore the gentle swaying motion of the craft, the sickly shifting sensation of the waves I haven't yet grown accustomed to. It's a stormy night on the lake and the winds churn the usually placid waters.

Quietly, so as not to wake my companions, I slip out of my hammock and draw back the tarpaulin over the doorway of our shelter. Cold wind and wet spray hit my face, whipping my hair wildly around me. Lightning forks through the sky, briefly illuminating the roiling clouds and the foamy crests of the waves. In the darkness that follows, I can just make out the shadowy shape of the docks we have drawn up against and the more distant silhouette of the walls of Selbius.

I try not to think of what, or who, lies within those walls. I don't want to remember where I've come from or what I've left behind. But, unbidden, a memory forms in my mind. The memory is of a brisk autumn day and a trek down a leaf-strewn forest path...

CHAPTER ONE

———◆◇◆———

I T WASN'T A LONG DISTANCE from the part of the forest where Rideon and the other outlaws were encamped to the old hideout of Red Rock. I followed an overgrown deer trail part way and when that faded beneath grass and leaves, trusted my sense of direction to lead me on.

I arrived before midday. Nearing the abandoned spot, I slowed, remembering the Fists would surely have an eye on our old lair. I circled the clearing, cautiously, noting the ground was freshly churned by horse hooves and the marks of many feet. Our enemies had come and gone. Scattered possessions, abandoned by the outlaws, were strewn across the ground. The Fists had been thorough in their ransacking, even burning clothing and provisions, presumably so we couldn't return later to reclaim them. I briefly sifted through the singed rubble, finding nothing salvageable.

Then I entered the cave. Feeling my way down its darkened passages was disorienting because nothing stood where I remembered it. A row of kegs and a lantern hooked to the rock wall had once marked the entrance to my space behind the falls, but they were gone now. I would have passed the spot by, if not for the roar of the water and the dim glow of daylight filtering through.

It was a relief to discover nothing here had been disturbed by the Fists. I went to my old hiding niche in the wall, dusted away the camouflaging bits of moss and pebbles, and retrieved the leather bundle containing my mother's brooch. Stuffing the parcel into my jerkin, I also collected the fistful of copper coins I had stashed in the hiding place. These were my only valuable possessions in the world and I breathed a sigh of relief at having them safe in hand again.

I lingered another moment, taking a final look around the quarters that had been my shelter for so many years. Then, turning to leave, I staggered into the silent figure that had crept up behind me.

CHAPTER TWO

"TERRAC!" I EXCLAIMED, MORE SHRILLY than I intended. I quickly modified my tone to one of disgust. "Have you been standing here spying on me all this time?"

"I have," he admitted, unabashed. "I looked for you last night but couldn't find you and again this morning, but no one had any idea where you'd gone. I followed my suspicions and the trail you didn't bother to cover and both led me here."

He looked around. "The place is a mess, isn't it?" he asked.

I frowned, still annoyed at my carelessness. "The Fists didn't tidy up after themselves, no. If you don't like it, feel free to leave."

He didn't take the hint. "Why are you here anyway?" he asked. "It had better be important. Rideon doesn't want us creeping around Red Rock, and I don't think he'll continue this new habit of letting you slide past his rules. He says the Praetor's men will be watching this place."

"Rideon says a great many things," I said. "But sometimes I need to follow my own promptings."

Terrac looked closely at me. "That doesn't

sound like you. You've always been quick to jump at his every whim, the first to defend each word from his mouth. Don't tell me you're finally giving up your misguided loyalties?"

"My misguided loyalties are none of your business," I said. "I'm just beginning to think a few things out for myself, that's all. And you can wipe that smirk from your face, because I'm not about to concede you were ever right."

"I'm not smiling."

"Oh yes, I forgot you're too good to gloat," I said. "Well, never mind. You've found me and now you can leave me alone. I've decided to go away for a bit to stay with a…" I hesitated to call Hadrian a friend. "An *acquaintance* in Selbius. I'll be gone a while, and I don't want you trailing after me."

"I've no intention of trailing after anybody." He sounded affronted and slightly hurt. "Aren't you even curious why I've been looking for you?"

"Not especially."

"I'm leaving too," he said. "I wanted to tell you farewell."

I hid my surprise. "Yes, well, save your tender good-byes until you've spoken with Rideon. I've a hunch he's not about to let you go anywhere. And we both know you'll never set foot beyond Dimming without his permission."

"Really?" Terrac folded his arms stubbornly. "Care to lay any wagers on that?"

"Since when does the pure-hearted priest boy take bets?" I teased, amused despite myself.

"You know, you're getting to be quite the rebel these days. One moment you're wagering, the next you're contemplating breaking your oath to Rideon. What would good old Honored Thilstain say about all this?"

He looked a little guilty but didn't back down. "Never mind my oath," he said. "Brig's death has made me rethink a lot of things, including my situation here. I've decided to find my way to Whitestone Abbey and the priesthood intended for me. These past few years haven't changed my destiny, merely delayed it."

"Well," I said shortly, "I hope you find peace at your Abbey, slaving over translations and prayers with your broken vow hanging over your head. For myself, I have my own plans, and it's time I put them into action. Farewell, Terrac."

He said, "You sound disappointed in me, Ilan. What makes you so concerned with whether I keep my word to Rideon? You yourself once told me honesty meant nothing to thieves and cutthroats."

"Never mind. Forget it," I said, unable to explain even to myself why I disapproved. Maybe it was merely his hypocrisy that irked me. Then, too, he was also holding up my progress. I moved to slip around him, but he intercepted me, grabbing my arm.

"I don't break my oath lightly," he said. "I'm running as far from Dimming as I can get, but not for the reasons you think. The truth is I'm afraid. Does that surprise you? Probably not. You've

6

always thought me a coward anyway and have never been slow to say so."

His tone turned bitter. "Well, maybe I'm not as brave as Rideon's loyal hound, but it's not my life I'm concerned about. Not this time. You want to know what I'm running from? Well, here it is and you can laugh at me if you like."

Despite his defiant tone, he was suddenly looking everywhere but at me. "This life—this world you've brought me into—it's changing me, and not for the better. I don't know what I'll become if I stay here. I've always valued truth and justice; you know that. I'm no Honored One, and maybe I'm not fit to be one, but I've still got to hold on to a bit of myself, don't I? I don't want to wake up one morning to find myself no different from the rest of you."

I thought he flattered himself with such a concern and was about to say so when his fingers tightened around my arm, reminding me he wasn't the weak boy he had been last spring. He seemed unaware his grip was cutting into me as he said, "What happened the other night at the woods holding... You remember how I found you?"

I nodded, reluctantly. It wasn't a scene I cared to think about.

"I saw you kill that man Resid," he continued. "I watched from the shadows, while the two of you struggled. It wasn't fear that held me back from aiding you. I was unwilling to involve myself in the violence, you understand?"

7

I did. Terrac had always deplored fighting.

"So I hung back," he resumed. "But suddenly, I saw that man nearly knock you over. I knew he was going to kill you right there, and I felt... Fear. A tide of fear and anger like I'd never known before. I was ready to join you then, although I had nothing to fight with but my bare hands. If I was too late to save you, well, at least I thought I'd find a way to avenge you."

The only part of his story I found particularly shocking was that he cared enough to avenge me, but I kept the thought to myself. I could see he needed somebody to hear him out.

He went on. "I was about to rush in when, suddenly, you recovered, slashed his throat, and as quick as that, it was all done. The fight was over and I hadn't even moved."

His gaze lost its intensity, but he still appeared unable to look at me. "I cannot tell you how horrified I was when I realized what I had been prepared to do. I would have murdered that man or died trying."

So that was it. I shifted uncomfortably, pointing out, "It wouldn't technically have been murder. Resid was a traitor who deserved to die."

"A traitor to you maybe and to your Red Hand, but so far as the law was concerned, he was assisting in apprehending dangerous criminals. So were those other men, the Fists I nearly burned alive in the hold house."

I didn't much care for this turn in the

conversation. "You can hate yourself over those Fists if you want," I said roughly. "I don't know how to keep you from it. But I forbid you to pity Resid. The scum betrayed Brig to his death and tried to kill me. Your only thought was to protect a friend—or to avenge one, as the case may have been. Both were worthy intentions."

"Worthy for mindless animals like Rideon and the rest of you, maybe," he said. "But not for me."

Now he was beginning to sound like himself. "Oh, dust off your grey robes, priest boy," I said. "You didn't kill Resid; I did. So feel free to go off to your abbey with a mostly light conscience, and spend the rest of your life brooding over the dark deeds you contemplated but never actually committed."

His expression cleared. "Then you agree I'm right to go?"

I said dryly, "I agree that you'll keep me here debating the question until I *do* agree, so let's cut the discussion short. Go to your abbey. Go with the blessings of Rideon, the band, and all the province."

He smiled a little. "Now you're giving away more than you have the power to grant."

"I'll give you the king's throne if you'll take yourself out of my way," I said, shrugging. "I've places to be."

He looked glad to change the subject. "What exactly are your plans?" he asked. "Has it anything to do with this?"

Before I could stop him, he darted a hand into

my leather jerkin to snatch the bundle containing the brooch.

"I saw you dig this out of your secret hiding place," he said smugly.

"Give me that," I snapped, roughly attempting to wrench it back from him, but he withheld it from my reach.

I said, "That parcel holds the brooch from my mother and it's important to me. Return it or I'll pound what little brains you have out your ears."

Instead of complying, he tucked the parcel into his belt, as if he intended it to stay there permanently. "Tell me why it's so important you get it back, important enough to risk returning to this place, and I'll give it back to you."

I glared. "I told you. I'm leaving the forest and don't know when I'll be back. I didn't want to leave behind anything of value."

"Except your outlaw friends. And me."

"Don't flatter yourself," I growled.

He said, "Look, what's the big secret? Why won't you tell me where you're going?"

I sighed and gave in. There was no need for secrecy, other than to annoy him, and that strategy was coming back to bite me. "Walk with me as far as the Selbius Road and I'll share a little of my plans," I said. "But first, let's put this place behind us. I don't think Rideon was wrong when he warned about the possibility of Fists keeping an eye on the area."

Terrac agreed and together we abandoned

the dark reaches of the cave for the bright outdoor sunlight.

We stepped into an ambush. The surrounding clearing was occupied by over a dozen armed men, outfitted in the black and scarlet of the Praetor's Fists. All stood waiting, weapons drawn.

Terrac and I froze. I had only seconds to take in our situation before a blurry object whizzed past my head, nearly nicking my ear. The Fist archer notched a second arrow to his bowstring and Terrac, framed in the mouth of the cave, tried to shove me back inside. Didn't he realize we'd be trapped like mice in there? I planted my feet, resisting movement, as my mind raced to form a plan—any plan.

The archer was prevented from loosing the next arrow when a sudden command split the air.

"Hold! I want these mongrels taken alive for questioning."

The order came from a broad-chested mountain of a man on horseback. Evidently the one in charge, he fixed a cold gaze on Terrac and me and commanded the others to take us up.

As the Fists closed in, I cast my fear aside. Sliding my knives free of their wrist-sheathes and pushing Terrac out of the way, I sent a blade flying to stick in the shoulder of the nearest Fist. Then I broke into a run, grabbing Terrac's sleeve and hauling him along with me. Together we darted for the nearest trees.

Unfortunately, a handful of men stood between

us and our escape. I dodged the first enemy, slipped a knife into the side of the second man moving to intercept me, but was less fortunate with the third, who caught my shoulder as I attempted to dart beneath his arm. Terrac came to my rescue, slamming into the Fist and sending him reeling backward. My friend didn't stop there but regained his balance and ran on, with me close behind.

Neither of us slowed on reaching the shelter of the trees. I ran as if my heels had wings and Terrac was faster still. A hail of arrows arced through the air, thudding into the ground around us. But the density of the forest worked in our favor, the thick trees shielding us and forcing our mounted enemies to rein in their horses and search for clearer paths.

I had no idea where we were going. My breath soon came in ragged gasps, my heart thudding painfully against my ribs. The ground began to slope, lending momentum to my weary legs. I stumbled repeatedly as the incline grew steeper. A fallen log leapt in front of me and, hurdling it, I lost my footing, crashing and rolling downhill. Brambles and saplings whipped at me as I cartwheeled down before finally slamming into a thick tree trunk.

The force of the collision knocked the breath from me and the treetops swayed dizzyingly overhead as I tried to find the strength to rise. I heard sounds of approaching men and horses and, looking upward, saw our pursuers not far behind. Ignoring the hammering in my skull and the burning of my lungs, I crawled to my knees and staggered on, letting gravity pull me down the incline. When I neared the bottom, a fresh storm of arrows whistled by, embedding themselves in the surrounding trees.

I skidded and stumbled on until the ground leveled out and a tall stand of shrubs blocked me momentarily from the view of my enemies. There, as if on signal, my legs gave way and I collapsed to the ground, where I lay panting, cheek pressed into the cool earth. In that condition, it took me a moment to notice the limp arm stretched across my field of vision.

Terrac! He was stretched out facedown and motionless. The rise and fall of his shoulders showed he was breathing, but an arrow protruded from his back and his tunic was stained scarlet. I had time to take in no more than that as I became aware of the sound of many feet crashing through the underbrush above. Urgency lent me the strength to drag Terrac's limp form into a tall stand of itch leaves and toadsbreath. My bow fell from my shoulder, clattering to the ground, and I dragged it out of sight also, before collapsing beside Terrac and letting the waving greenery close over us.

I flattened myself to the ground, trying to quiet my noisy breathing, as I heard the Fists' arrival. They scattered to search for us, but I knew they wouldn't have to look long. I glanced at Terrac beside me. His eyes were closed, his face smeared with blood and dirt. Twigs and leaves stuck out of his hair. With his sun-browned skin and ragged clothing, nothing marked him apart from a common woods thief. No one would mistake him for a young priest-in-training anymore. Remembering how his strange, violet eyes had captivated me at our first meeting, I felt the urge to save him now as I had then. But this time I was as helpless as he.

The crack of a stick underfoot betrayed an approaching Fist. *This is it,* I thought. *Time to face death.* But there was no question of giving up without a fight. My hand fumbled for my bow. I had no arrows, but it was my only weapon, so I gripped it tightly, wondering at the calm washing over me the moment my fingers closed around the lightwood.

A whisper of movement passed through the air overhead. Unthinkingly, I threw myself to one side, narrowly avoiding the descending blade aimed at my head. I scrambled upright, swinging my bow out to whack my attacker across the knees. The Fist only grinned at my ridiculous maneuver and swung his blade in what would have been a disemboweling sweep, if I hadn't managed to avoid it. The sharp tip of the steel only licked the skin across my stomach, but I immediately felt the sting of the shallow cut.

More enemies joined the first, fanning out around me. I backed away but was acutely aware every reluctant step carried me farther away from the injured Terrac. With my friend lying prone on the ground and me creeping backward like a cornered rabbit, the Fists evidently remembered that it was preferable to take me alive. They crowded in tighter, and I spun in a circle, impossibly attempting to keep my eyes on all of them, while brandishing my bow before me like a club.

Some of my opponents laughed and I realized how pathetic I must look.

"Nice staff you have there, thief," said one of the Fists, a short, bearded man with curly hair. "Now why don't you just put it down and surrender?" His voice wasn't unfriendly and he appeared to take it for granted I would do as he asked.

When I didn't immediately respond, he asked, "Got any more knives up your sleeves?" and took a measured step closer, as if testing my reaction.

"Come on, Bane," one of his friends encouraged. "If she had any more, she'd have used 'em by now."

Emboldened either by that observation or by my hesitation, the man called Bane moved nearer still. I darted a quick glance behind me, but there was nowhere left to run.

Bane seemed to read my thoughts. "Don't even think about it," he said. "Our archers would drop you before you go six paces. But we don't want to do that—not unless you leave us no choice. You heard our captain. He wants you alive so he can ask a few questions."

"I don't doubt he does," I said. "You caught several of my friends the other day and I saw their condition when you were done questioning them."

Another Fist grinned. "So you found the bodies, did you?" he asked. "We hoped you would. Think of it as a little present from all of us. That'll be the fate of every one of you thieving scum before we're through. The Praetor has sworn to it."

Bane waved him to silence and said to me, "If you saw what happened to your friends, you know some of my comrades can get overzealous in their work. You'd be wise to throw yourself on the mercy of our captain while you can. If you don't, I'm afraid you won't be all in one piece by the time he arrives."

He nodded toward Terrac's motionless form. "Anyway, look how far running got your friend. It doesn't have to end the same way for you. The captain is a fair man and he might let you off easily on account of your youth. So why don't you lay down your weapons and come along with us? We'll take you straight to him and the two of you can talk things over."

I hesitated. You could never trust a Fist, but what choice did I have? Even as this man spoke, he'd been sidling closer until he was only an arm's length away. Suddenly, he was reaching for me.

In the same instant, my bow grew hot in my hands, startling me so badly I nearly dropped it as it flared to life, shedding a brilliant fiery light. Simultaneously, I felt its powerful presence awakening, not just in the bow itself, but somehow inside my mind.

I shook my head against the disorienting sensation, even as I saw the Fist grabbing for me, and darted out of his way. Another enemy took a swipe at me and I narrowly evaded his sword. Bane shouted at the others to hold back, but he must have seen, as I did, that the game was over. He couldn't control his companions, and I wasn't about to stand there and let them kill me.

I feinted to one side, the nearest enemy moved to intercept me, and I dodged the other direction, diving through the opening he had left.

Free at last, I flew through the trees with renewed energy, hearing my enemies scrambling after me. They were mere steps behind—the nearest had only to stretch out a gauntleted hand to touch me. But Brig used to say I was the fastest runner he ever saw, and I tapped into some new source of strength now. I had no idea from where it came. I only knew that the distance between the Fists and me was widening. Remembering the archers, I ran in a zigzag pattern, putting as many trees between their bows and me as possible. My unnatural speed compensated for the lost ground and the gap continued to grow.

As soon as I was out of view, I dropped into a cluster of weeds, allowing my pursuers to pass by. Then I ran on in the opposite direction, never slowing. The scrape across my belly burned, where the Fist's blade had scored my skin, but the pain drove me on. Returning to the outlaw camp was impossible, not when it could lead the enemy to our door. Instead, I raced toward the setting sun, relieved when I began passing familiar landmarks. All of Dimming was home, but there were parts I knew better than others, and I was coming onto safer ground.

The sun had sunk behind the trees and the first stars were twinkling in the evening sky when I splashed into the shallow waters of Dancing Creek. I slogged downstream, following the pull of the swift current as it swirled and capriced over stones and around fallen logs. The creek bed was slick with moss. Thousands of tiny pebbles shifted and skittered beneath my boots, and then the stream deepened and I found myself wading through pools of murky, green water up to my thighs. A little distance farther and the creek shallowed at a section of rapids. The current was so strong here it pulled me off my feet more than once. Always I scrambled up and hurried on. I was exhausted by the time I reached a place where the creek split into two smaller streams. I took the least obvious one and pushed on until I was waist-deep in a pool of stagnant water. I could go no farther.

An immense tree grew along the bank, its spreading roots stretching out to skim the water. I ducked under the slimy surface, swam beneath the tangle of roots, and emerged within their embrace, pressing into the muddy bank to conceal myself. There was a sort of large animal den burrowing from the water's edge up beneath the tree and, unslinging my bow, I shoved it into the tunnel and pulled myself up after. My feet were left dangling in the water. It was unnervingly dark and I tried not to dwell on the possibility of the wild creature that lived in this den returning. Or worse, of the Fists finding me trapped and at their mercy.

But even these fears couldn't hold my thoughts for long as, strength spent, I rested my cheek in the gritty mud and allowed my eyelids to droop. My last conscious action was to shove the unnerving bow as far from me as I could. It had stopped glowing, but I could still feel its presence in my head, as I succumbed to sleep. Strange, soft murmurings of the thrill of battle and the sweetness of blood whispered through my dreams that night.

CHAPTER THREE

THE FOLLOWING MORNING I AWOKE to find myself still free, or as free as anyone could be trapped deep in a burrow beneath an old elder tree. It was no easy feat wriggling out of the muddy hole and dragging my bow out after me. I still seemed to hear the echo of its voice from yesterday, insinuating thoughts of violence into my mind. It was cold to the touch this morning and lifeless as any other bit of dead wood, but I hadn't forgotten how it glowed during the fight, throbbing with a life and strength of its own. As soon as it was safe, I promised myself I would be done with the thing, would cast it off to rot someplace and try to forget its disturbing effects. But for now, I needed to hold onto it a little longer.

Under the light of day, I was troubled to remember I had lost my mother's brooch. I had last seen it in Terrac's possession and with his capture, it too was lost to me. The severing of this final connection to my past was a blow, but I couldn't focus on it now. I had other problems to occupy my mind.

I examined the shallow cut across my belly

inflicted by the Fist's blade yesterday. It was less painful this morning, and I didn't think it would take long to heal. After rinsing my injury in the stream, and breakfasting quickly on a handful of berries, I set out.

It was still in the early hours of the morning when I left the creek behind me. Sometime during the night I settled on a plan. I didn't know whether Terrac still lived and if he did, what tortures he could be suffering even now at the hands of his captors. But I had to find out and I had to do it alone. Rideon and the others would want no part of what I had in mind.

My purpose firm, even if I had no idea how I would carry it out, I made time as quickly as I could, knowing Terrac may have little of it to spare. Although I sacrificed stealth for speed, I attempted as I walked to keep a wary eye out for enemies and was grateful when the woods around me appeared to hold no one but myself and the occasional bird or squirrel.

In this way I traveled for two days, until I left the shelter of Dimmingwood and stepped out into open country. Here, I found before me vast rolling meadowlands, such as I had not seen since my childhood. The low, green hills stretched as far as the eye could see in every direction, save the one from which I came. Unaccustomed to so much open space, I felt vulnerable and unsettled by the scarcity of bushes or trees. Still, I had to forge ahead. Terrac needed me.

With the forest at my back, I set my face toward Selbius, where I believed the Fists would be taking Terrac. I had no delusions about what I was doing. Selbius was the Praetor's city and I was walking into the jaws of the lion. My only hope was that I might have help when I reached Selbius. If I could find the priest, Hadrian, perhaps he would be familiar enough with the city to offer me guidance in locating Terrac. I tried not to think any further ahead than that.

It was late into the evening of my second day when I spotted a collection of rising green humps in the distance that I recognized from other people's descriptions as the settlement of Low Hills. This marker told me I had only a few more miles before I would be within sight of Selbius. If I walked all night, I could arrive there the next day.

My legs rebelled at the thought and for the first time in my life I found myself longing for a horse to ride. In Dimming, my own feet had always been good enough, but with the stretch of land I had yet to travel and my gnawing anxiety driving me forward, I felt I could not get to Selbius quickly enough. Tomorrow was the first day of Middlefest, and I hadn't forgotten Hadrian's invitation to rendezvous at the Temple of Light on that day. If I arrived too late, my chances of finding him in the strange city were small.

So I pushed weariness and aching muscles to the back of my mind and kept my feet moving until I came upon a broad, straight highway. Here, there was a weathered signpost with arms pointing in three directions, one indicating the way to Kampshire, another to the provincial border with Cros, then to Black Cliffs and on clear to the coast. I ignored both these and followed the third option, which would take me to Selbius.

I traveled for a time, feeling uncomfortably exposed beneath the bright moonlight. There were no shadows to conceal me, no hint of any cover, except the occasional bramble bush growing along the side of the way. I was acutely aware anyone coming up the road behind me would have a full view of me long before I had any idea of their presence, but I tried not to dwell on that. My muffled footsteps were loud in my ears and I longed for the familiar creak and rustle of treetops swaying overhead. Even the noisy chirrup of tree frogs would have been welcome just then.

But I didn't have to suffer the stillness much longer because by the time dawn's pale light streaked the skies, I began encountering other traffic. When I sighted the first wagon clopping in from the opposite direction, I dived into a low ditch at the side of the road and hid until it passed by. Not much later, a group of travelers herding a train of pack animals approached from behind and caught me unawares. It was too late to conceal myself for they must already have seen me. So I forced myself to march woodenly onward, face turned straight ahead. No one so much as glanced my way as they passed, so after that I didn't bother leaving the road again, but put on an innocent face and tried to look like any law-abiding citizen who had a right to be where I was.

As the morning wore on, the sun grew hot and the air thick with dust kicked up by the long string of traffic now winding down the road. I was nearly run down several times by horse and wagon alike, so I quickly learned to keep to the road's edges. It didn't take me long to feel how conspicuous I was among these people. Noticing none of the other travelers approached a state as filthy and bedraggled as the one I was in after my recent experiences fleeing the Fists, I stopped long enough to smooth my hair back into a tidier tail and to wet a portion of my tunic with my tongue, using it to swipe at my dirty face. My clothing was beyond help, but I straightened my jerkin and rolled up the muddy sleeves of my tunic, by way of improvement. That didn't stop the next person to pass me, an old man with a cart full of potatoes and blackroots, from directing a suspicious stare my way, as though he thought I was going to steal the pitiful contents of his cart.

I grinned cheekily back at him and raised my hands to show they were empty.

"Useless woods folk," I heard him mutter as he drove on.

I shrugged at the unprovoked insult and kept walking.

"First visit to the city, is it?" said an unexpected voice nearby. I started because I hadn't noticed the black-haired young man falling into step alongside me. He followed close behind a passing wagon, which seemed to be part of a long train winding its way toward the city.

"What makes you think I've never been before?" I asked. I was a little tired of passersby looking at me as if I were a toad crawled out of the woods.

The young man appeared unoffended by my tone. "Well, if you had, you'd not be returning to it. You'd know by now why woods folk avoid Selbius. It's not the safest of places for your sort. I'm Jem, by the way. Jem of Low Hills. I'm one of Banded Beard's merchant guards."

I ignored the introduction, not offering my own name. "I never said I was one of the woods folk."

"No, but you are just the same. I can recognize you people on sight. You gawk at everything like you never saw daylight before and jump at every stranger who gives you good morning."

I tried to hide my nervousness, grateful his assumption had taken him only halfway to the truth. Better to be thought a woods villager than be recognized for a forest brigand.

I said, "You talk as though woods folk have cause to feel unwelcome in the city. Why is that?"

He shrugged. "There's some as always suspect your kind of looking for trouble or anything to steal. Woods folk have a reputation for causing a stir."

At my expression he said, "But cheer up, friend. No need for the fierce scowl. You're not in trouble

25

yet and you don't need to be. No reason for the guard to single you out."

"Guard?" I asked, my head snapping up. "What guard?"

"You have been in the woods a while, haven't you?" he said. "There's always a handful of city guardsmen keeping an eye on the gate, at the call of the Gate Clerk. He has a table to one side, where he records the folk coming and going and what goods they bring in and out."

I groaned, stopping in my tracks, and Jem had to haul me aside by one arm to save me being run over by a passing wagon.

"I've told you, there's nothing to worry about. Might be a good idea, though, to keep moving before we get ourselves trampled."

I allowed him to drag me forward as he continued. "I'll help you out," he said. "There's no reason anyone should look twice at you up at the gate. Woods villager or not, you haven't done anything wrong."

If he only knew. Still, I was grateful for the aid he offered.

"Why should you help me?" I asked. "You don't even know me."

"I know you enough. I've cousins in one of the woods villages and if they were to come to the city, I'd want a stranger to give them a hand. Now then, here's the trick. The city guard don't care much for woods folk, so if they recognize what you are, you'll be lucky to get in the gate. It's a situation that calls for a little deception."

As he spoke, he shrugged out of his long grey coat.

"Here," he said. "Slip this on over your clothes until we're past the gate and stick close to my master's wagons, as I do. Doesn't nobody want to bother a merchant's guard, even if you look a little young for the part."

I was hesitant about the plan, but he was already shoving his coat at me and I didn't want to attract the attention of other passersby by wrestling the coat back and forth. Slipping the bow from my back, I handed it to Jem while I wriggled my arms into the long sleeves of his coat. I pulled the front closed over my deerskin jerkin and instantly felt less conspicuous in the crowd.

Jem looked satisfied. "There. Now you look like an ordinary farm hand, low on work and hired out to watch trader's goods. That's my story anyway."

I nodded. I thought he had more the look of a farmer than a fighting man.

He said, "Just act confident and casual and no one will notice anything amiss."

"I don't know how to thank you for this," I said.

"You can repay me by not giving our little pretense away. Now, as to this bow..." He hefted the weapon. "This marks you plainer than deerskins. Let's tuck it into the back of one of my master's carts until we're through the gate."

He quickened his steps enough to catch the wagon ahead and in a moment the bow was stowed safely away, concealed between rows of barrels.

Somehow having the bow even an arm's length away felt too distant, but I told myself not to be foolish. I hadn't had the weapon very long and there was no reason to suddenly feel so dependent on it.

Selbius came into view long before we were anywhere near it. In a land this barren and treeless, the city was visible for miles in any direction. At first, I could scarcely make out the looming grey walls in the distance for the blinding glare of the sun glinting from the surrounding waters. Jem told me Selbius meant, in the tongue of our ancestors, a house built over water. The name was apt because the entire city had been constructed over a small isle in the midst of a vast lake. It wasn't one of the larger cities of the kingdom or even the largest one in the province, I knew, but to me it seemed immense. I thought there must be many thousands of people packed within the great granite walls.

Another of Selbius's impressive features was the long bridge spanning the water, making the city accessible from shore. Seeing my interest, Jem told me how the city was built by the present Praetor's great-grandfather during the peak of the Coastal Wars.

He said, "I've heard the ancestors of the house of Tarius were a seagoing people, so maybe that's why they decided to settle over water. They still carry on a few strange customs within those walls that don't come from any of our provincial traditions. But be warned, the city's not as impressive inside as it looks from here. Selbius has got its pretty districts with their terraces and pools and walled gardens. Not that such as you and I would be welcome to linger in those places. But like any town, it also holds its dark and squalid areas. Take my advice and stick to the marketplace and the common district."

"Are ordinary folk not allowed elsewhere, then?" I asked.

"We're free to wonder where we please, as long as we don't engage in illegal or disruptive activities, but there are parts of town that can prove dangerous to those as don't belong in them. Like the under-levels or the old docks outside the city walls. Even the guard doesn't venture around those places, unless they've good reason to. As for the wealthy areas, they're not forbidden, but if the guard see you there, they'll speculate on what trouble you could be planning and that's not the sort of attention a newcomer like you needs."

"What are the under-levels?" I asked, curious.

He grinned. "You really don't know anything, do you? Listen, we haven't got time for me to tell you about every part of Selbius. Even if I knew all there was to know of it, which I don't. This is all you really need to know. We're going to cross the bridge in a little bit and arrive at the trade gate on the other side. There'll be a few guardsmen there and they'll make some minimal effort at questioning every tenth person in line. So long as nothing unusual comes up, you'll be in." I wanted to ask what sort of unusual things might come up and what would happen to me if they did, but he was already rushing on.

"Once you're beyond the gates, you'll find the curfews and codes of conduct for the city posted regularly in public places. Familiarize yourself with them and before you so much as toss an apple peel onto the street, find out first if it's permissible in your district. The Praetor's a strict one for laws. Which reminds me, don't take the curfew lightly. Let the city guard catch you roaming the streets after sundown and, unless it's a holiday or you've another pretty good reason, you'll be arrested and spend the night in the round house."

"Sounds to me like these city people invent an awful lot of senseless rules," I said.

Jem shrugged. "The Praetor has a tight hold over his city and, while he may not be the most popular of rulers, no one's denying he keeps good order. Hasn't been a murder within Selbius's walls in three years. That brings me to another thing. Thieving in the city will get you more than a whipping and a day in the stocks. For a first offence, you'll lose a hand, for the second, you'll be hanged. That's the Praetor's feeling on second chances. His Fists are even less forgiving, and they're always looking for an opportunity to prove they're more efficient than the city guard, so you'll want to step shy of them if you can. They're a rough lot."

"So I've heard," I said, keeping my expression unreadable. A guilty thought popped into my head and I had to ask, "Am I endangering you and your company? I mean, if it's discovered I'm smuggling my way in."

He laughed. "Forget it; it's been done before. Anyway, being a woods villager isn't a crime—at least not yet. If you're found out, I'll play ignorance and my master will suffer a light reprimand from the Gate Clerk for not watching over his party. Don't know exactly what would happen to you, but how much trouble can you get into for pretending to be what you're not?"

I wasn't eager to find out, as we crowded onto the end of a slowly moving line shuffling across the bridge. The next half hour dragged by as our line snaked forward one foot at a time. I was unaccustomed to being crammed into close proximity with so many people and I quickly began to feel stifled and hemmed in. Things got a little better once we were out over the lake, where the shadow of the bridge fell over the surface of the green water. A refreshing breeze off the lake carried away the unpleasant smells around us and dried the sweat on my face.

As soon as I had the opportunity, I squeezed over to the bridge's edge. Looking down over the side, I could see schools of orange-skirted fish floating to the surface to snatch at insects before darting back into the depths. A long-legged blue-

31

fisher was wading in the reeds near shore, in search of an easy meal.

"What are they doing back there?" I asked Jem, pointing to a collection of dark-skinned men laboring along the inland shore. They appeared to be loading large hunks of rock onto log rafts and floating them out toward Selbius's island.

"Some older parts of the city are under reconstruction now," Jem said. "Those chunks of granite were hewed from the quarries near Kampshire and have been hauled miles overland to get this far. The men ferrying the rock to the island are river people. Drawn by the Praetor's promise of gold, they've abandoned the rivers and come with their rafts to help the Praetor's workmen move building materials back and forth between Selbius's island and the mainland. The work goes more quickly with their expertise and the use of their rafts and river barges."

I remembered Hadrian mentioning having friends among the river people, so I wanted to ask Jem more questions about them. But the line was moving forward again and we had to hurry to get back to our places behind the last wagon of our train before the space was filled by the press of bodies. As we approached the wide gates at the end of the bridge, I observed the row of guardsmen Jem warned me about, lining the entrance. I saw a narrow-faced fellow with the sun glinting off his bald head, sitting behind a small table to one side of the gates. He didn't wear the armored uniform of the city guard, but a ceremonial-looking blade hung at his waist and a scarlet band encircled his upper arm, denoting a position of authority. He could be no one else but the Gate Clerk. Jem confirmed this, explaining to me that this man served a unique role as a former member of the guard who had retired with merit from active service. I nodded, observing the thick ledger open before the Gate Clerk. As each citizen passed his table, the clerk threw each a quick question and recorded their answers into his book. Then he would wave an impatient hand and bark for the next to step forward.

The guardsmen lining the gate mostly kept out of the way, except to urge on anyone who slowed the progress of the line. They didn't appear particularly interested in any of us as they joked quietly among themselves and shuffled about, obviously bored with their duty. I thought I could have dragged a siege engine up to the gate and they wouldn't have noticed.

As we approached nearer, I could hear the dry voice of the clerk as he questioned each individual. Usually, it was the same dull exchange.

"What business?"

Fruit vender, or cloth merchant, or basket weaver, along with the citizen's name, was answer enough to earn entrance.

Jem bent to whisper near my ear. "Don't forget; we're with Banded Beard, a dealer of wines and spices. That's all you have to say."

33

"Spices, wines, Banded Beard." I muttered to myself, committing the instructions to memory. When my turn came to stand before the table, the bony clerk didn't even look up.

"Business?"

"I'm with him." I mumbled, jerking my head toward the back of Jem's master, who had already passed through.

"How's that? Speak up, girl!" The clerk demanded impatiently.

"I work for Banded Beard. The business is trade." I winced at how loudly the words came out.

The Clerk looked neither accepting nor doubtful. "In what do you trade?" He asked, his pen hovering over the ledger.

A trick question? Banded Beard had already spoken for us. If the Clerk bothered to test me, didn't that mean he was suspicious? Nervously, I caught Jem's eye. He nodded his head slightly, as if to reassure me. I swallowed and answered, "I safeguard the goods: spices and wines."

That felt too abrupt, and in my eagerness to think of something to lengthen it, my nervous tongue got away from me. "You won't know me; I never came to the city before. Usually, I just hire out to work on the farms, but this year my Da thought—"

"All right, all right, I don't want your life's story, girl. Give your name and quit clogging the line." At his words, a pair of lurking guardsmen took a step forward. I needed no further encouragement.

Hastily, I ransacked my mind for a good, likely name. Nothing came to mind and it seemed to me the few seconds' silence dragged into minutes.

"Ada," I said at last, out of desperation. The Clerk bent to record my name and I stumbled quickly away after Jem and the wagons.

I repeated the name over in my mind as I stood behind Banded Beard's wagons, waiting for the folk ahead to trundle through the gates. Ada. What had possessed me to take up my mother's name? It didn't matter, of course; it wasn't as if her name was known here. I was only borrowing it for a time. Still, it felt strange speaking a name I hadn't heard used in so long. Our line moved forward and I followed the stream of wagons and traders, passing through the tall, ironbound gates and into Selbius.

CHAPTER FOUR

I F I WAS SURPRISED BY the press on the bridge,
I was stunned by the number of people milling
around inside the city's walls. The gates
opened onto the edge of the market square, and
I could scarcely see beyond the moving crowds
to the shops and houses of timber and stone
spreading beyond. All was noise and confusion.
People jabbered, animals brayed, and a high-sided
wagon loaded with squealing pigs passed by so
near it splashed muddy water across my boots.

"This is where we part ways," Jem told me,
yelling to be heard over the commotion. "Remember
to keep your wits about you, your hands in your
own pockets, and avoid the city guard. Watch your
possessions and your company and you'll be fine.

I thanked him for his help, retrieved my bow
from his master's wagon, and gave him a few
coppers in exchange for his worn coat before we
parted company.

The streets were crowded the day before
Middlefest, and my progress was slow as I pushed
my way through the press. I told myself the
crushing throng was to my advantage because

even with an ordinary coat to cover my deerskin clothing, I felt conspicuous walking the streets with the bow on my back. No one else around me appeared to be armed, and I was mindful of Jem's warning against attracting attention to myself and my origins. I only hoped with so many strange visitors in the city for the holiday, no one would notice one more peculiar sight.

There were certainly plenty enough other odd looking strangers to draw the eye. I saw folk from Cros mixed in with the crowd. They stood out among our local people for their drably colored clothing, the strange forked beards of their men, and the broad, floppy bonnets of the women.

I saw Camdon visitors, conspicuous by their rich, colorful fabrics and long, open-front coats that swirled around their ankles as they walked. All the Camdon folk wore the stiff, high-necked collars and thigh-high boots fashionable in that province and the customary rings in their ears. Many of the women had a series of dangling ornaments punctured in rows all the way up both ears. They were the first women I saw in Selbius wearing breeches, though theirs were highly impractical, cut of fine fabrics and richly embroidered up the legs. There was a constant chiming whenever they moved for the multitude of tiny bells they wore sewn onto the cuffs of their boots and breeches. There was an old saying—'rich as a Camdon beggar'—and I could see now where it originated. Even the common folk of that province adorned themselves as vainly as our nobles.

Once, I also caught sight of a man of Kersis in the shifting crowd, attired in their rough mountain garb. Did they celebrate Middlefest where he came from? I would have thought the practical folk of the mountainous province would find our holiday too frivolous for their tastes. An axe dangled from this man's belt and a coat of wolf pelts rested across his broad shoulders. Folk made way for him as he passed through the crowd, and I was no exception. Craning my neck to follow his progress, I walked into a vegetable stand, jarring the table so that several purple onions rolled off onto the cobblestones.

After smoothing things over with the annoyed seller, I hurried on with less attention to the crowds and more mind to where I was going. I lingered in this part of the market just long enough to discover a stall where anything could be purchased, from copper washtubs to rugs, weapons, and herbal cure-alls. Here, I replaced my lost throwing knives, grimacing because the new ones I bought were far inferior to those I owned before. I had considerably less coin when the transaction was over and left the stall with the distinct feeling I'd been cheated. Still, it was made up for by the comfort of knowing I had a pair of sharp knives tucked up my sleeves once more.

After this, I pushed my way free of the thickest part of the crowds and abandoned the market place. The noise and commotion had me so confused I could scarcely think, and I wandered lost for a time before finally finding my way to a wide entrance letting onto a broad avenue cutting through the city. It seemed to be a main street, judging by all the pedestrians and carriages. There was more order here than in the market and most of the folk passing me moved with a quickness and purpose that kept traffic flowing easily. I wondered if the city was always this crowded or if it was due to preparations for the coming holiday. Either way, I was already missing the peace and space of Dimmingwood.

Where was it I was supposed to meet Hadrian? At a temple of some sort, but what was the name? The Temple of Light? Allowing myself to be carried along by the current of flowing bodies on the street, I scanned the rooftops on the horizon, hoping to see a spire or bell tower rising in the distance to guide me. Instead I saw nothing but slate rooftops and smoking chimneys. I stopped before the open door of a wine shop, where a weathered old man in a broad-brimmed hat sat atop an upturned keg, smoking a long-stemmed pipe.

"Begging your pardon, grandfather," I said. "But might you know the way to the Temple of Light?"

The old man pushed back his hat and squinted up at me. "You must not be long in the city or you'd know it yourself. The temple is a landmark around here. I suppose you're one of them what comes for tomorrow's festivities?"

"Actually I'm more concerned with finding

a friend, a priest of the Blade, whom I've an appointment with at the temple tomorrow."

He pointed a long finger at me. "Take my advice and be there early enough for the start of the celebrations. Be on the temple grounds at dawn, when the bell rings to mark the start of the holiday. I never missed it when I was your age."

I smiled. "I'll do that, but first you'll have to point me in the right direction. I want to stroll past the temple today and fix the spot in my mind so I can find it more easily in all the confusion tomorrow."

The old man nodded sagely and provided directions. Thanking him and committing the instructions to memory, I went on my way. Following the direction of the East Bridge as he had advised wasn't as easy as it sounded because there were buildings and walls in the way, and I had to take a series of detours down side streets and around shops and warehouses. Taller structures rose to block my view and twice I lost my guiding point so completely I had to retrace my steps to the last place where the bridge had been visible.

It was approaching evening when I finally found the Beautiful district I'd been told to look out for, and I estimated I had only hours left to find the temple before dark. I hadn't forgotten Jem's instructions on city curfew but didn't have time to stop and look for any of his signposts. I would just have to complete my task as quickly as possible.

I approached a low, arched entrance in the gray stone wall stretching before me and stepped through to find myself in another world. The Beautiful district was well named, an island of serenity hidden away in the heart of the bustling city. A series of colonnaded walks cut through the gracefully landscaped gardens, hedges lined the walks, and flowering vines cascaded down sculptures and trellises. Strange trees I had never encountered before shaded the gardens, their slender branches curled and intertwined into shapes as artful as the surrounding statuary.

I stepped onto the nearest cobbled path, my footsteps ringing loudly through the tranquil surroundings. The splashing of a multitude of stone fountains, together with the whisper of the breeze rustling through the greenery, seemed more natural here than my echoing tread, and I felt like a clumsy intruder in this peaceful place. Great basins of water were arranged on either side of the path and large golden fish darted about in the bowls, their movements disturbing the surface reflection of the evening sky. As I walked, strains of muted conversation and laughter fell upon my ears from beyond the hedgerows.

My path led me to a small roofed porch with no walls but a circular row of stone columns, half covered in creeping vines. Here, tiny moonkisses fell among the spray of greenery, their pale petals glistening like dewdrops in the waning light. A pair of lovers huddled on the stone bench within, and seeing they would not welcome my interruption, I let my feet turn onto one of the narrower side paths. The singing of the crickets in the hedges reminded me time was slipping by and I had yet to accomplish what I came for.

The old man at the wine shop had instructed me to look for the statue of Queen Tamliess, but I must have passed a hundred statues already. Reasoning the likeness of a legendary queen should be large and prominently placed, I quickened my steps, hurrying up one path and down the next, until at length I broke into an open area.

Here was a wide cobbled yard with carved benches lined in tight rows to form a half circle, as though folk occasionally came to hear a lecture or view some sort of performance. The yard was empty now but for a handful of citizens out for an evening stroll, and I would have hurried on had not my attention been caught by a flash of color at the far side of the yard. A paradin pen. I paused for only a second to watch the enormous strutting birds fanning their colorful tailfeathers, but in that brief glance, I caught sight of a towering statue beyond the pens. I ran to the spot and stood looking up at Queen Tamliess's image raised atop a wide pedestal, her famous winged crown nestled atop her head.

I put her to my back, as instructed, and hurried the opposite direction. Evening was fast overtaking me and as the light from the sky faded, the glimmer-stones beneath my feet began to glow. They would radiate soft light until the last of the day's heat had seeped from the stone. The gathering darkness reminded me how little time I had left to accomplish my objective and make my way back to any kind of shelter for the night before I would be violating city law. I certainly didn't care to be caught out after curfew if it would earn me the animosity of the city guard. But I decided I had just a few more minutes to spare, if I was quick.

I saw what could be the cemetery I'd been told to watch for at the end of the gardens and I set off in that direction, moving at a good clip. Hurdling over a low hedge, I hoped no citizens or city guardsmen were around to observe my suspicious haste. I barely checked my speed in time to avoid slamming into a stone wall on the far side of the hedge. I skidded to a halt. On the other side of this wall should lie the city's burial grounds and from there, if I had been informed correctly, I would see the temple.

I trotted along the wall until I found a low back entrance, but on ducking through the archway, my heart sank in disappointment. I didn't know what this place was, but it was surely no cemetery. The ground was paved with great squares of stone, and stretching on a great distance to either side of me was an immense flat pool of water, obviously manmade. Walkways skimmed the dark water and pond lilies rested motionless on the surface.

I walked past benches and great urns overflowing with sweet smelling flowers but no longer felt I was in any sort of garden, for this atmosphere was solemn and eerie. I stepped to the edge of the shadowy pool, but the water was too dark for me to make out the bottom. Carved hunks of granite and statuary rose to break the surface of the black waters and in the failing light, I made out words and dates inscribed upon them. I wondered what sort of monuments these were and the possible answer unsettled me. Hadn't Jem said the city's inhabitants held to strange old customs? If I looked down on these waters in the light of day, perhaps I would see row upon row of stone coffins resting beneath the surface.

My gaze settled on a rising spire soaring above the far wall, the highest structure I'd seen since entering the garden district. Could it be the temple? I cut across the cemetery, taking one of the crosswalks spanning the water, and tried not to think about what I might be walking over. Making my way to the nearest archway, I took the first path I stumbled on. Here, there were more people around, and I had to slow my steps lest I attract unwanted attention. The slower pace scarcely mattered to me for I was on temple grounds now.

The Temple of Light rose above me, its tall spire jutting into the sky, and the temple grounds, dotted with trees and small flowerbeds, spread to either side. I imagined this would usually be a serene and solitary place, but this was not the case on the eve before Middlefest. The pebbled courtyard and grassy lawn sprawling beyond were filled with bustling folk making preparations and setting final touches on the decorations raised for the holiday. Bright ribbon streamers and flower garlands festooned trees and lantern posts and an enormous bell had been drawn up to hang suspended from a temporary wooden frame in the middle of the yard. It stood silent now, presumably waiting to ring in the holiday tomorrow.

I paid scant attention to the preparations going on around me. I found what I sought and would be here to meet Hadrian in the morning—along with perhaps hundreds of other people. I decided not to think, for now, about the difficulty of finding a lone man in such a crowd. That was a problem for tomorrow. For tonight, the last pale light of day had nearly faded from the sky and with the descending darkness, my thoughts were heavy with the concern of avoiding arrest until morning.

But where could I spend the night? I had few coins in my pocket and didn't know if any inn would accommodate me for so little. My experience of the wide world, I was beginning to realize, was woefully small. Still, I must try. I took a straight, cobbled path leading out of the garden district and into a more populated area. Timber houses with slate roofs sprung up on either side of the road as I hurried on, until I came to a signpost that told me I was in the Commons now.

I didn't see anything that looked like an inn. Maybe if I could find a busier street? I ran on, setting my face in the direction that seemed to lead deeper toward the center of town. The further I went, the filthier and narrower the streets grew, until I was forced to wonder if I had taken the wrong way. There was no question in my mind I was traversing one of those dangerous areas of the city Jem had warned me about. It felt like a long time since I had passed anything but empty taverns and dark warehouses. It was now full night, and I slowed my steps, reluctantly giving up hope of finding an inn where the keeper would still be awake. I would just have to find an out of the way spot to sleep out the night, avoiding the guard patrols until morning.

But I wouldn't do that here. I didn't like the feel of this place. The streets were stinking and the looming warehouses made me feel hemmed in. I was about to turn back the way I'd come, when I became aware for the first time of quiet footsteps approaching me from behind. I felt a tingle up my spine. Was it the city guard or a footpad stalking me? *Probably just some drunk wandering home from the taverns,* I told myself. Nevertheless, he moved stealthily for a drunk. I stopped and knelt in the street, pretending to tighten my bootlace, while casting a surreptitious glance down the long way behind me. It appeared deserted, but I trusted my instincts, which told me I was being watched.

I rose and continued my walk, neither hastening nor lingering, until I came to the mouth of a narrow alley behind a row of gray sheds. Sauntering around the corner until I was lost from view, I ducked backward and pressed myself against the rough wall of the shed. My heart was pounding as I listened and waited and my hand moved to my sleeve to touch one of my sheathed knives. I wouldn't draw the weapon yet. I just needed to feel it there.

It's nothing, I repeated to myself. *Only a drunk, only an innocent passerby.* The knife handle beneath my fingers steadied me as I strained for any out of place sound. I heard nothing. No one passed by my hiding place. Maybe they turned onto a different path or entered one of the dark buildings. I counted slowly to a hundred before pulling my hand away from my knife and starting back for the mouth of the alley.

I hadn't gone two steps before a looming shadow separated itself from the wall down the far end. I started, not just at the unexpected movement, but at a sudden stirring inside my head. No more soft whispers. The voice of the bow was loud and distinct this time.

Yes! Blood! Death! Let me kill for you!

I flinched and yet, compelled by an instinct not my own, my hands reached for the bow. *Why am I doing this?* a confused part of my mind demanded. It was the knives I should grab for, not the bow.

I had no chance to sort out my thoughts and in the end it didn't matter what I reached for, because my hand never found either weapon. There was a whisper of movement across the alley and with no more warning than that, something solid and fist-sized flew through the air to strike me across the brow. I felt a swift rush of pain and then a sea of black was rising up to claim me.

CHAPTER FIVE

I AWOKE TO THE CRASHING BOOM of thunder and a dull throbbing in my skull. My dark surroundings were unfamiliar, and it took me a moment to recognize the alley where I lay sprawled across the cobblestones. As I sat up, clutching my aching head, it all came rushing back to me. The attack in the alley. The blow from an unseen enemy. Looking around now and casting my magic sense out like a net, I discovered no sign of my attacker.

I groaned as another boom of thunder sounded. The last thing I needed, as I huddled in the cold and dark with a splitting headache, was rain. Not when I had nowhere to take shelter for the night. I climbed to my feet, the motion setting my head spinning and forcing me to pause and lean against the near stone wall until the dizziness passed. Pushing aside the discomfort, I tried to figure out how long I'd been unconscious. Not long surely, for it was still dark.

I glanced uneasily into the shadowed mouth of the alley and wondered if my attacker was lying in wait for me out there. But no, whoever it was, they could have killed me easily while I was out cold, if that was what they wanted. Knowing that didn't stop my hands moving of their own volition toward the knives tucked up my sleeves. They weren't there.

Dismayed, I patted frantically at my sleeves as if I could make the weapons magically reappear and scanned the ground at my feet, sensing already the action was a futile one. It didn't take me long to find my pockets had been emptied as well. There seemed something stupidly ironic about my having fallen victim to a footpad, but at least I could be relieved it had been nothing worse. I wondered what my outlaw brethren would think of my clumsy mishap in the big city and immediately determined they would never hear about it from me.

Thoughts of Rideon and the rest reminded me what I was doing in Selbius in the first place. It was time to find Hadrian and get back to my mission. Dusting myself off, I resettled my clothing and smoothed my hair, re-knotting it in a sleek tail down my back, before stepping out of the alley. At least the thief had left me in possession of my coat and bow, either because he was in a hurry or just not too hard up.

I was startled by another ear-shattering clap of thunder overhead and a bright flash of light. But when I glanced skyward, it wasn't shards of lightening that met my eyes, but thousands of multi-colored sparks raining down from the sky. A second volley of sky-fires followed, coming from the direction of the garden district. I was too distracted to admire their magnificence. Why had the Middlefest celebrations begun so early? The sky-fires shouldn't have started until tomorrow evening.

The answer that came to me was one I didn't like. Had I been out all through the night and the following day? It was possible. I had known men to sleep for days after a blow like the one I received. But if I'd missed the dawn celebrations, I had also missed my meeting with Hadrian. My heart sank, but I refused to accept defeat so easily. I set off briskly down the street, clinging to the faint hope I might still find the priest among the celebrants there. What other options did I have?

As I made for the Beautiful district, I kept a watchful eye out for the city guard, because even if curfew had been banished for the holiday, as it apparently was, I still wanted to avoid attention. For that matter, I didn't need any further encounters with street thieves either. But I needn't have worried. The streets of the common district were nearly deserted, and I encountered only a handful of citizens hurrying, like me, toward the gardens.

I followed the path I had left by the previous night and emerged around back of the temple to find the grounds crowded. The other day I had thought the marketplace teeming with bodies, but that was nothing in comparison to this. I had never seen so many people. They spilled out of the temple grounds and into the gardens. The entire yard was motionless, enveloped in awed silence, as every eye but mine followed the impressive display of sky-fires being engineered from an upper terrace of the temple.

I viewed the scene in the eerie light of the illuminations. Tables had been set up around the grounds, many holding food, others kegs of ale or enormous bowls of punch. I passed stands selling glimmer-stones and flowery wreaths for half-pennies. It was clear the vendors of the city didn't miss a chance to profit from the holiday. As I pushed my way through the crowd, I earned angry looks and muttered curses for treading over the feet of whoever got in my way—which was pretty much everyone. But I couldn't care about courtesies tonight, not when I had only one thing on my mind. Finding Hadrian. I scanned the crowd for a large, dark-haired man in gray robes, but finding the priest among this mass of humanity felt like a hopeless task. Clambering up a low half-wall at the yard's edge to get a better view over the heads of the crowd, I studied the audience.

Once, I caught the flash of a gray robe, but when I looked closer it was only one of the temple priests, ducking through the crowd on some errand. When at length, the sky-fire display ended and the crowd began to mill around, it became impossible for me to see anything. A handful of rowdy youngsters came, shoving and crowding me for my spot atop the wall and I gave it up without a fight. It was clear I wasn't going to find the priest like this anyway.

I shoved through the press again, even more difficult now the crowd was in motion, and fought against the stream of people slowly pouring out of the yard. I emerged at the front steps of the temple only to find the doors were shut against the late hour and I couldn't gain admittance. After making a final circuit of the grounds, I gave up in despair and left the grounds to wander off into the gardens.

I walked past the water cemetery and the paradin pens and the tall statue of Queen Tamliess. Someone had set a garland of ivy leaves atop her crowned head and small candles glowed in her cupped hands and within the carved niches of her skirts. More candles ringed her feet, and she seemed almost to come to life beneath their flickering glow. The sight briefly distracted me from my disappointment. I walked the gardens, breathing in the heady perfume of the elfblossom and maidenseyes and taking in the scenery. Tamliess wasn't the only statue adorned with garlands and candles. The gardens were aglow with warm, flickering lights illuminating the night long after the last light of the glimmer-stones underfoot had faded. Distant sounds of music and laughter drifted on the breeze, mingling with the splashing of fountains and the singing of the crickets.

A sudden cry split the serenity. "Stop, thief!"

Startled, I whirled around but couldn't make out where the shout came from. *How have I been discovered?* I wondered in a panic. And who was my pursuer? Then, an indistinct figure came barreling around a corner and into my vision. The person was little more than a blur in a blue coat as he dashed down the footpath and, before I had time to react, dodged past me to dive into a hole in the near shrubbery.

The bushes had barely closed behind him when two large men, bearing pikes and wearing what I guessed to be the uniform and half armor of the city guard, bounded into view from the direction he had come from. Still shouting, "Stop, thief!" and "Surrender in the name of the Praetor!" they looked momentarily confused at finding their quarry had suddenly vanished.

Skidding to a halt, one of the guardsmen, a rough looking fellow with a reddened face, demanded of me, "Did a suspicious looking man in a blue coat come running through here?"

I tried to appear casual, but it was difficult, being so close to men in the Praetor's employ. These guardsmen were only a step away from being Fists and it was the Fists who had taken Terrac and would be glad to get their hands on me too if they guessed what I was. My mouth went suddenly dry.

I shoved my hands in my pockets to hide their shaking and, maybe as an act of defiance against my fear or maybe for some other reason, answered, "Yes, he ran that way." I nodded toward one of the off-branching paths.

The pair ran away in the direction I indicated and it wasn't until they were out of sight that my pulse slowed to a normal rate and my palms stopped sweating. Even knowing they weren't after me, the close encounter was an unsettling experience.

"Pssst," a low voice whispered from the shrubbery after the guards were gone. The bushes rustled and a single eye peered out at me through a hole in the greenery.

"Thank you, friend," the stranger said. "I don't know why you meddled on my behalf, but I'm very glad you did."

"Forget it," I said. "I wasn't trying to help you so much as to spite the city guard. Any men under the Praetor are enemies of mine."

"Ah, a fellow lawless after mine own heart," he said. "I take it we share the same trade?"

My hesitation must have given away my reluctance to answer the question because he seemed to realize his mistake quickly.

"Forgive me, I shouldn't have asked that. Trusting strangers is a luxury not everyone can afford. I should know."

At that moment, angry shouts and the sounds of returning footsteps alerted us the guardsmen were returning.

"I'm afraid that's the sound of your spiting coming back on you," the stranger told me. "They must have discovered your ruse. Quickly, come with me."

I hadn't intended to become this deeply involved,

but it was too late to think of that. I scrambled into the bushes after him and, motioning me to follow, he started quickly off down a twisting path through the hedges. It didn't take me long to realize he was leading us through a sort of maze. The rows of shrubbery grew tall as we went, soon reaching higher than my head, and the sounds of our enemies faded in the distance. The green labyrinth wound inward like a coiled snake and we followed the circular course, bypassing frequent openings that led down alternate paths. My strange companion never faltered. It was clear he had a particular destination in mind.

After a short walk, we stepped into a clearing I guessed to be the heart of the maze. Here stood a tiny, low-roofed pavilion and a wide pool of water with a stone sculpture at its center.

"Nimble thinks we're safe here," my companion told me, coming to a stop. "Most people couldn't find this place, but I know the garden district, or for that matter, all of this city, better than the city guard."

"Who's Nimble?" I questioned.

"My partner in crime," he explained. "He has a talent for picking up things other people miss, so I consult him in everything."

He slipped a hand into his coat pocket and withdrew a wriggling, fist-sized creature whose brown fur grew in mangy patches and whose scaled tail was half the length of its body.

I quirked an eyebrow at the ugly animal. "Your

partner is a rat?"

"The cleverest helper I ever had," he assured me, settling the creature on his shoulder, where it looked perfectly at home. "He never argues, never betrays, and always gives sound advice."

Suspecting the rat of being a convenient instrument for his owner's opinions, I said, "And right now *Nimble's* advice is...?"

"Sit and wait," my companion answered. "Few and determined are those who find their way to the heart of the Beautiful."

"I expect the determination of the guardsmen will depend on the value of whatever it was you stole," I said.

"When you put it that way, they might consider a long search worth their while, yes. A certain noble woman is missing some particularly fine jewelry up on Round Street tonight. Luckily, no one saw my face."

"All the same," I said. "I'd be eager to leave the vicinity if I were you."

He said, "That's because you're not using your head. I'm not about to be picked up on the street with stolen goods in my pocket. Much better to lie low for the night and slip away in the morning, after the searchers are long gone. That's my plan anyway, and I advise you to do the same."

So saying, he dropped to the ground and pulled off his boots. For a moment, I thought this was his preparation for going to sleep, but then he began pulling the legs of his breeches up to the knee.

Unable to contain my curiosity any longer, I had to ask what he was doing.

"Isn't it obvious? I'm wading," he said, stepping into the shallow pool in front of the pavilion.

"At a time like this you're going to play in the water?" I asked.

"I'm not playing at anything. I'm securing our good luck by placing a coin in the mouth of the water nymph," he said.

As he spoke, he splashed to the center of the pool where the likeness of a playful water nymph wrapped in her long hair crouched among the lily pads. Her parted lips, revealing a collection of shiny coppers inside, indicated this sort of offering was a common tradition for the few who made their way to the heart of the maze.

My companion added his offering to the rest, before splashing his way back to me. I noted that, despite his precautions, his breeches were soaked to the knee, but he didn't complain as he climbed over the edge of the fountain to sit at my side. Clearly, he considered the relative discomfort worth the gain.

When he finished tugging his boots on again, he led me to the covered pavilion where we found a pair of long benches set against the walls. I gathered these were to serve as our beds for the night. The space was narrow, the floor no more than a dozen steps across, and the towering columns weren't as sheltering as solid walls would have been. But I told myself that was just as well because if our enemies discovered us here, we would have several quick routes of escape.

Leaning back on the cold stone, I found the roof overhead was as insubstantial as the walls. Just a set of crisscrossing narrow beams, over which grew a tangle of intertwining vines. I stared up through the open patches of greenery into the starry night sky and thought of Terrac. I was surprised to feel loneliness washing over me, as I wondered if I would ever see him, my outlaw friends, or my forest again. Dimmingwood seemed a thousand miles away from this strange city. My mind moved to Hadrian and my failure to locate him. A thought occurred to me.

"Thief?" I called softly into the darkness.

The shadow sprawled across the opposite bench lifted his head. "You called?"

"Yes, I just had a thought."

"Savor that novelty. Some of us are trying to sleep." Despite the words, his tone wasn't unkind. Encouraged by that, I said, "I've thought of a way you could repay me for aiding you earlier."

I heard his yawn. "Did you aid me? I've already forgotten. Besides, I think I remember you saying something about the joy of crossing the city guard was its own reward."

I ignored that.

"I came to Selbius looking for a certain man," I said. "He was supposed to be at the temple at the start of the Middlefest celebrations this morning, but I missed our meeting. If you care to repay your debt, you can do it by finding this man for me."

I half expected a careless refusal, but he surprised me by remaining thoughtfully silent for a moment. At length he said, "Selbius is a good-sized city. What gives you such confidence in my ability to hunt this fellow down for you?"

"You've boasted that you know Selbius better than anyone. I'm giving you a chance to prove it."

"How generous of you. I suppose I probably could find your lost man at that, but why should I want to?"

I was growing irritated. "Because you owe me a favor and you know it," I said. "I've made enemies of the city guard, not a wise thing to do around here, in order to save your sorry hide. Already, I begin to regret it. Will you help me or not?"

He sighed and said, "Very well. I'll set to work finding your precious friend in the morning. Now, will you stop nattering and let me rest in peace?"

Satisfied, I said, "Thank you, thief."

He lifted his head again. "You can't go around calling me that in public, you know. I might as well wear a thief's brand on my forehead."

"You don't seem to want to give me a better name to call you by," I pointed out.

"Well, I guess it doesn't have to be my real name." He thought briefly. "Fleet. I go by that one now and then. Yes, you can call me Fleet."

"I'm Ilan," I introduced myself.

I expected an acknowledgement from the thief, but Fleet remained silent, and after a moment, I decided he was already asleep.

I hadn't enjoyed a real sleep, without the aid of the footpad's blow to my head, since arriving in Selbius, and my weary mind and body were both begging for rest. I allowed myself the luxury of lying down and closing my eyes but tried to keep my ears open and my senses attuned to the night around me. Somehow, despite these efforts, I drifted into a light sleep and dreamed of death and blood, all the while vaguely aware of another consciousness nudging its memories into my mind. I tossed and turned until my hand came to rest on my bow.

CHAPTER SIX

I AWOKE AT DAWN'S FIRST LIGHT. As soon as my eyes opened, I sprang upright on my stone bench. How could I have been careless enough to fall asleep? I looked around for my companion of last night, only to find he had deserted me while I slept. Rot that piece of street filth; he had promised to aid me! I immediately felt around for my bow and breathed a sigh of relief when I found it. At least he hadn't taken that. Snatching it up, I scrambled to my feet and out into the gray light. The air held the chill of early morning and the sun was just rising to burn away the mists.

There, at the edge of the dew-streaked lawn, paced Fleet. He was tossing a pebble back and forth in his hands, eyes fixed on the ground at his feet, but was instantly aware of me the moment I stepped out of the pavilion. He ceased his pacing to watch my approach.

"Contemplating abandoning me in my sleep?" I asked suspiciously.

"Only a little," he said. "But now you've taken that decision out of my hands. I thought you'd never be up. You sleep like a corpse."

I snorted for answer and took the opportunity to study my new acquaintance under the light of day. He was shorter than me, despite appearing a few years older. Lean and wiry, he had a narrow face and lightly tanned skin, wore his dark, greasy hair slicked back in a tail, and sported a scrap of whiskers on his chin that was closer to a shadow than an actual beard. A prominent jaw, altogether too long, was his most noteworthy feature. He was dressed in a slightly faded, tight-fitting coat that might once have been fashionable and wore a thin strand of cheap, false gems strung close about his throat. A similar stone dangled gaudily from one ear.

I wasn't sure what to make of a street thief who dressed as vainly as a Camdon merchant, but the incongruous sight made me smile.

Fleet caught my expression and said with a knowing gleam in his eye, "I see you appreciate a good thing when you see it."

I couldn't tell if he was jesting, but I said, "Actually, I was thinking you remind me of a fat, strutting paradin decorated in shiny baubles."

"Fat?" His eyes widened in alarm.

"Well, maybe just when your feathers are fluffed." I reassured him.

He shrugged. "Your opinion is the minority, I can tell you. The ladies aren't at all opposed to my preening. But you'll see for yourself soon enough, I shouldn't wonder. I'll grow on you."

"Like stink-moss?"

He frowned. "Never mind me. Look at yourself, woodlander. I can practically see the leaf-mold growing between your toes."

I became alert. If there was one thing I didn't need in this town it was to be associated with the woods folk. I'd heard enough about that danger already.

Fleet must have seen the concern on my face. "Never mind, woodchuck," he said. "It isn't that obvious and your coat helps. Just pull your hair down loose and keep that bow out of sight. Walk with less confidence, like the city women do, and you'll pass well enough."

But he continued studying me. "If we could only get our hands on the right clothes, I could turn you into one of those wild mountain women from Kersis. Folk would be afraid to stare at you too hard then."

"I'll pass on the costume," I said. "Just make me inconspicuous. That's all I ask."

I slung my bow over one shoulder and he helped me arrange my long, gray coat to conceal it. I looked a little hunchbacked when we were finished, but Fleet said it wasn't too noticeable. At any rate, I wouldn't be parted with the bow, so I had little choice. I also pulled my silvery hair free of its tail and combed it with my fingers.

"Not bad," Fleet said of the effect. "I could almost imagine you pretty, if it weren't for that horrible crooked nose."

"I got it in a fight with an arrogant paradin who

talked too much," I said meaningfully.

He changed the subject quickly. "I'm famished. What do you say we go looking for some breakfast?"

By midmorning we sat concealed behind a low wall backing the market square, devouring the juicy red berries and slices of sweet waterfruit Fleet had deftly filched from a fruit vender's stall. I hadn't realized how long it was since my last meal until I sank my teeth into the fruit and felt its sticky juice dribbling down my chin. It was good to lean against the sun-warmed wall at my back and relax with a full belly. But comfortable though I was, I didn't forget Terrac was probably enjoying a less fortunate state. I had to save him and to do that I must enlist Hadrian.

I gave Fleet a short explanation of how a friend of mine had been taken up by the Fists and of why I hoped locating Hadrian would lead to a plan for freeing Terrac. I told him all I knew of the priest and the only clues I had for finding him. I told him also of my misfortunes the night before Middlefest, of how my falling victim to a footpad had prevented my making our rendezvous in the temple, to say nothing of costing me a new pair of knives and a handful of coin. Then I recounted to him Hadrian's reference to the river people.

When I was done, Fleet frowned and pursed his lips thoughtfully.

"River people, huh? Makes a body wonder what

sort of priest this friend of yours is, that he has dealings with those folk. Not many do. Certainly not priests of the Light." He chewed his lower lip. "Still, you're determined to find him, and I guess if this is our only clue to his whereabouts, I can manage it. Should be easy enough to get out to their river rafts. I just don't know how we'll be received when we arrive. I've heard they're hostile to strangers. It's about the only fact anyone knows about them. I should also warn you I don't speak a word of their twisted dialect, so we may have a bit of trouble making our questions understood."

"But you'll come with me?" I asked.

He grimaced. "Ah well, I've taken worse risks. Who knows? Maybe it'll be an adventure."

I wasn't looking for adventure. Rather, I was fervently hoping after this was all over my life would slow to a duller pace for a long, long time. I kept these thoughts to myself and asked instead, "Exactly how do we go about finding these people, Fleet?"

"There's no finding to it," he said. "You must have seen them on the old docks as you crossed the bridge into the city. That's where they stay. Never come inside the city walls. They're no more welcome here than... well, than we'll be when we enter their community."

"I'll take my chances," I said, scrambling to my feet. "Let's be off."

"Not so fast. There's one little matter I have to take care of first. In case you've forgotten, I still carry certain borrowed goods on my person, and I'll be more comfortable after I've got them out of my possession."

I couldn't conceal my impatience. "What are you proposing?" I asked.

"Nothing that will take up much of our time," he said. "I've a friend who turns stolen goods into gold. Come on." And with no more explanation, he led me off.

I tried to ask where we were going but could get little information out of him.

"Nowhere pretty, I'll tell you that much. Not a place you'll want to be seen coming and going from either. The city guard watch you closer if they think you've got business with the folk down there, so I keep my visits to a minimum. But there's no help for it today."

I shook my head in confusion, but he didn't seem to want to disclose anymore. I was beginning to learn my strange companion enjoyed a mystery.

I said, "Well, wherever this secret place of yours is and whatever your friend does there, I hope you don't expect me to pay for any part of it. Don't forget I was robbed and haven't a copper left to buy myself a penny-loaf of bread, let alone to purchase your friend's services."

Fleet was unperturbed. "Who spoke of purchasing, I'd like to know?" he called over his shoulder as he threaded his way down the crowded street. "I don't believe in paying for things. This is a simple business arrangement, a case for bargaining, and luckily I've the chip for it. Just settle back and leave everything to me."

The under-levels were a warren of underground tunnels of stone and clay reaching like dark, spreading roots beneath the clean city streets above. The tunnels had been constructed as part of the previous Praetor's plan for a complex drainage system for floodwaters and city waste, Fleet told me. The endeavor had proven a failure either for inadequate planning or lack of funds and work on the tunnels had ceased years ago. Now they provided a filthy dwelling place for citizens too impoverished to afford shelter elsewhere, as well as a dank, smelly hideaway for disreputable types who didn't wish to conduct their business under the light of day.

I was unsurprised to find the entry to the levels located in the beggar's quarter of the Common district. Fleet led me unerringly to the mouth of the entrance, slid aside the metal grate, and together we descended the winding steps leading into the bowels of the city. The light was dim here but by no means dark as night. Occasional glimmer-stones were cemented into the walls along with the building stones and these provided an eerie, greenish glow to illuminate the levels. I would have paused to wonder how those stones stored and emitted light underground without the sun's rays to replenish them, but in this unnatural place such a small phenomenon seemed unremarkable.

I suddenly felt very far away from the bright sunshine and bustle of the world above. An odd silence hung like a shroud around us, and the very air we breathed was stale and stifling. When we came to the foot of the steps, we found ourselves in a high-ceilinged open chamber from which numerous smaller tunnels branched off in various directions. I caught sight of a few ragged children scurrying off like rats down those side tunnels, but this wider chamber appeared to be the most heavily inhabited area.

Before me spread a haphazard collection of hovels, shoved against one another in close, disorderly fashion, their walls made of any kind of unwanted rubbish the inhabitants had been able to get their hands on. A few homes had dirty blankets strung across open doorways to provide a measure of privacy, but most entrances stood open to the outside. There were no roofs on the dwellings, probably because the chamber ceiling overhead already provided shelter from the elements.

Many of the shacks leaned against other structures for support so that there was little room for walking between them. There were no discernible paths or rows to keep to, but following Fleet's lead, I picked my way carefully along. Those inhabitants who had not raised hovels or tents over their heads sat or sprawled heedlessly over the stone floor, often crowded so tightly together I could scarcely move without stepping on them. A full half the folk we passed were sleeping, despite the early hour of the day. I supposed down here in the dark, they did not mark the hours of the days and night as we did above.

My attention was drawn to the many pitiful folk who were ill. They coughed and shivered, half naked and often lacking even a thin scrap of blanket. I felt a mixture of sympathy and unease at the sight. It hadn't been so long since the years of the rotting plague and I thought nervously what a prime breeding ground this place would be for such diseases. I noticed that Fleet, ahead of me, avoided touching anything around him and I followed his example.

Many of the inhabitants of this depressing place watched us with disinterest or not at all as we passed, but our arrival caused a small stir among others. A handful of unfortunates clutched at me, begging for a coin or two, until they learned I had nothing to offer. Fleet, with his gaudy jewelry and finer clothing, drew beggars like a loaf of honey-dipped bread. But I noticed, though they followed him like hopeful dogs trailing their master, none put out even a tentative hand to touch him. They relied instead upon their pitiful cries to capture his sympathy.

For his part, he appeared not to hear them. I wondered what it was that made these people so wary of my companion when they didn't hesitate to tug at my arm or attempt slipping their hands into my coat pockets. Then I remembered Fleet was not an uncommon visitor here. Perhaps he had proved himself less than patient with such attempts in the past.

The wariness of the beggars notwithstanding, by the time we reached our destination, we led behind us a short, ragged procession. Fleet stopped before a shack of rotting timbers that was the sturdiest dwelling I had yet to see in this place and the first to boast a real door in front. At this point, Fleet whirled suddenly on his heel and drove the lingering beggars away with curses and threatening gestures, until they scattered back the way they had come. Then he turned back, straightened his coat, and rapped softly at the door, careful, I noted, lest it fall off its hinges.

In a moment, he was rewarded by the door being cracked slowly open. The man who peered out at us was heavy set and greasy haired and wore an unwelcoming scowl as he thrust his round face out the door. Then, apparently recognizing Fleet, his face broke into an ugly smile.

"Davin." Fleet greeted him coolly.

"Why, Fleet, my lad! I have not laid eyes on your ugly face nor heard mention of you in months. I was beginning to think the iron-heads had caught you at last and given you your just deserts at the end of a noose. But there've been no hangings in town recently. So I says to myself, 'maybe Fleet thinks he's too good to cross the threshold of his old partner again.'"

Forgetting I'd yet to be introduced, I jumped

into the conversation, demanding sharply, "You say there've been no hangings lately? You're sure of that?"

My mind had naturally flown to Terrac.

The big man frowned at me. "Believe me, I know when there's a hanging afoot. Always look to see if it's one of my old friends dangling."

He turned his attention back to Fleet. "Who's this young companion of yours with such interest in hangings?" he asked.

Fleet waved a hand, as if to indicate I was no one of significance, a response I found vaguely insulting.

"Just a friend," he said. "But we didn't come to chat over old times and past crimes. I have business for you."

The fat man's eyes took on a greedy gleam.

"I do not, however, have any intention of discussing it on the doorstep," Fleet said. "Are you going to invite us into that hovel of yours or keep us standing out here with the vermin?"

The fat man hesitated, flicking a suspicious glance at me.

"She comes with me," Fleet said firmly. "I trust her and that should be good enough for you."

The fat man shrugged before stepping back to hold the door wide.

"Any friend of Fleet's..." he said with unconvincing grace.

Fleet shot me a quick glance I couldn't read, but I thought there was some sort of warning in it.

I suddenly realized how much he was trusting me with. The contacts and secrets of his trade. For a thief, that was no light thing and I hoped the look I retuned said I would honor his trust.

I ducked my head under a low beam as I followed Fleet into the shadowy interior of the hovel and for the first time in my life found myself regretting my height. It was usually an advantage to be as tall as most men, but right now I was discovering a definite downside. The ceiling here was low and I had to keep my shoulders hunched and my head bowed, a burden neither Fleet nor the fat man had to bear.

The first thing which came to my attention immediately after entering the fat man's hut was the fetid stink in the air, a mingled scent of ale fumes and old urine with maybe a bit of rotting garbage thrown in for variety. I choked back my initial desire to return to the comparatively fresh air outside and tried to distract myself by examining my surroundings.

The hut was lit by the glow of a flickering lantern that did little to banish the shadows or to reveal what lay beneath them. Scattered around was a collection of broken furniture and rubbish, crammed so closely into the tight space there was hardly room to turn around without stumbling into something. Large earthenware containers and bulging canvas sacks were stacked along the walls in heaps as high as I was tall. I suspected them of being filled with old clothes, cheap jewelry, and any other loot Davin could get his hands on. From what I could see of the goods, they were not the sort of thing our band back in Dimming would have bothered stealing. I privately wondered how much of the accumulated treasures Davin had filched from the unfortunates camped around his hut.

Davin noticed my perusal of his home. "Admiring my collection, I see," he said. "Doubtless you're wondering what a man of my obvious success is doing living down here amongst the filth."

I couldn't decide whether he was being ironic.

He continued. "Well, I'll share a secret with you, young woman. It is not my means which keeps me huddled below ground like a sewer rat. I chose this spot to lurk because it is the only place in Selbius where one can be entirely free of the eyes of the cursed city guard. Rotting iron-heads, always sniffing around up there; won't give an honest thief a moment's peace."

Fleet was nodding sympathetically.

"Down here, below level," Davin said, "it's nice and quiet, and I can work in secret without the law keepers looking over my shoulder. But I am rattling on like a slack-jawed old woman. Come, come, sit and rest yourselves at my warm hearth and we'll talk business."

There was, in fact, no hearth or if there was it was hidden behind piles of debris, but Davin led us to a slightly less crowded corner, picking his way through the jumbled rubbish with surprising agility for such a large man. He seated himself in a sagging chair, the only sturdy looking bit of furniture in the place. I was just as glad to remain on my feet. Fleet, seeming unperturbed by the squalor or perhaps merely accustomed to it, pulled up a wooden keg and sat down.

"Now," Davin began, "you say you came to discuss matters of the trade—" He interrupted himself suddenly to shout over his shoulder. "Heslan, I cannot discuss business on a dry throat!"

He smacked a hand loudly on the arm of his chair. "Where are you woman? Bring us a drink!"

I hadn't noticed any other presence in the room, but at his call I became newly aware of a shadowy figure moving in a darkened corner. An emaciated woman, well past her better years, clambered sluggishly up from a filthy tangle of sleeping rugs on the floor to follow Davin's bidding. Her long, greasy hair spilled untidily over bony shoulders, bared by a loose, low-cut blouse. She moved with an unsteadiness that suggested she'd been sampling from the bottle she brought to us. She also fetched us three chipped, dirty mugs before fading again into the shadows.

"All right," Davin said when she was gone. "I'm ready to discuss this proposition of yours, Fleet."

He poured both our mugs full, setting his aside. I noted how Fleet held his drink untouched until he saw the fat man himself take a swig from the bottle.

"Don't be so hasty, my friend," Fleet said, leaning forward. "Before we discuss any new endeavor, I think it would be wise to settle any business remaining unfinished between us."

Davin looked innocent. "I don't know what you mean. I can think of no unresolved matter."

Fleet smiled thinly. "Then allow me to refresh your memory," he said. "There was a job six months ago on Merchant's Row. As I remember it, I was cheated out of my cut and I mean to settle that oversight now."

"Do you?" Davin said, his expression confident. "Then let me give you a piece of advice, lad. You don't want to do anything foolish. I shouldn't have to remind you of some of the... not so pleasant people who count me friend." He leaned forward and, though his voice never lost its friendly tone, his eyes were distinctly cold. "Don't try to blackmail, badger, or otherwise coerce me into or out of anything, lad. Certain of my acquaintances might take exception."

Fleet's expression didn't alter, but I caught the sense of dread washing over him. Whoever these friends of Davin's were, they were evidently not anyone Fleet wanted to come up against. I sensed him struggling with something, possibly hardening his resolve.

He said, "I think we're both equally aware of the sorts of friendships you curry, Davin. I don't doubt you could order me tortured or dismembered in any way you liked and it would be done by nightfall. But let's ask ourselves what would be the benefit of doing away with an old friend when he has come all this way to bring you business he could easily have taken elsewhere?"

The heavy man laughed suddenly, a deep throat-clearing noise that fell harshly on my ears. "I see, I see. You come to bargain," he said. "Do you really think you're sharp enough to concoct any scheme that would tempt me into parting with my money? After all these years you should know better."

I could see the mockery was getting to my companion. Fleet's composure cracked enough for his hand to move, as if of its own accord, to his coat sleeve, where a faint bulge betrayed the presence of a knife. The move wasn't lost on Davin, but the big man only laughed again.

"You cannot think to threaten me?" he asked. "You must realize I don't fear you one wit, but you persist in showing your teeth, like a fox cornered in a hunt."

Fleet flinched at the words, as if aware of a hidden meaning. "And am I being hunted?" he asked quietly.

It seemed a strange question to me, but Davin's face immediately sobered.

"Not yet, boy. You're lucky that I like you, despite many of your stupider actions, past and present. I haven't set your name on any death list, and I won't, so long as you don't force the issue. But I'm warning you to forget this debt nonsense and be satisfied to keep your neck. What would you have done with your share anyway? You'd have drunk and gambled it all away inside a week's time."

"What I do with my money is my own business," Fleet said. "I thought the glitters I've brought today would interest you, but now I see further dealings between us would be a mistake. I cannot trust you with such a valuable opportunity."

Davin frowned. "Glittery goods, you say?"

"The best. I've never wasted my time or yours with cheap baubles."

"Doubtless you're exaggerating what you have, but just the same, you've stirred my interest. Would it be out of the way for me to ask to see these shinies?"

"Naturally, I wouldn't expect you to buy what you haven't seen," Fleet said, as he fumbled inside his coat and withdrew a knotted kerchief. When he untied the small bundle to display a glittering brooch and a pair of ear ornaments studded with blood-red gems, I felt my eyes bulge and saw Davin's do the same.

"No wonder the chase last night," I muttered. Fleet shot me an annoyed look and I realized he was telling me to keep my mouth shut. Clearly he didn't want to talk about the source of these jewels in front of Davin.

The big man reached for the gems, a greedy gleam in his eye, as he asked, "How'd you have the good fortune to get your grubby hands on these?"

Fleet snatched the jewels beyond his reach.

"Sorry, trade secrets," he said. "What you should be asking yourself is how you might persuade me to part with them. To start with, I'll be wanting to settle that old debt we just discussed."

Davin waved a careless hand, his smile calculating. "That small coin? Of course, it's yours. That's if these jewels prove to be the real thing. But you cannot expect me to put a value on the stones before I've been allowed to examine them. How do I know they're not cheap imitations? Any fool can polish a bit of red-rind and pass it off as heartsfire."

Fleet's expression was cool. "The lady who possessed these was not the sort to have her jewel box graced by pieces of red-rind. All the same..."

He considered the jewels briefly before tossing the brooch to the big man, who caught the ornament deftly between thick fingers and held it up to his eye. When Fleet had brought a lantern close, the two leaned over the brooch. Davin's expression had grown serious and it was clear he was in his element. He pried the jewel loose from its backing and lightly scratched the back of the stone with a thin blade removed from his belt-pouch. Grunting to himself, he then held it up to the light, flipping it over.

"It's real enough," he finally concluded.

"Yes, of course it is. Didn't I say as much?" Fleet demanded impatiently. "And something else I know is what stones like these are worth, so don't think you're getting the better of me on this deal. If you want them, I expect you to meet my price, or I can easily take them elsewhere."

Davin snorted. "Methinks you've an overblown opinion of yourself and your find, street thief. We both know you haven't the contacts to unload these gems in a market where they won't be recognized, and I don't think you want to be caught with them in your hand either. You're as eager to be rid of them as I am to purchase them, so I'll give you exactly what I gave you last time and you'll have the sense to take it."

The big man nodded at me. "Tell our friend here to think things over before he makes any hasty decisions."

I had no opportunity to respond, as Fleet climbed to his feet to glare down on the other man. "You're a filthy snake, Davin," he accused. "A sloppy eel with the brains of a—"

"Now, now," the heavy man interrupted. "I take it by the abuse you're leveling that you've come to see the light of reason. You can leave off the litany and just thank me for taking the rocks off your hands."

"I want the money inside the week," Fleet said sullenly.

"Of course you do," Davin agreed, gathering the other jewels from the kerchief. "Come now. Drink another round with me before you go and let's put this nasty bargaining business behind us."

Fleet said, "You know, considering how you're robbing me on this deal, the least you could do is seal our bargain with a gesture of good will. You might, say, throw in a pair of daggers for my friend here. She's lost her old weapons, and we all know how unpleasant it feels to go without."

Davin shrugged, saying, "I'm sure I can find something lying around that will suffice."

Fleet tipped me a wink when the heavy man wasn't looking and I realized he wasn't displeased with the outcome of our visit but had probably planned all along for it to end as it did.

CHAPTER SEVEN

THE OLD DOCKS WERE NOTHING more than their name suggested, rickety structures outside the city walls, hiding beneath the shadow of the spanning bridges leading into Selbius. It was obvious at a glance the stone and timber structures hadn't stood up well to the effects of time. What decades of lapping water had been unable to erode, sun, weather, and woodborers were not far from finishing. There were great gaping holes in the wooden planks and even the sturdier parts of the dock creaked so alarmingly beneath our feet, I half expected the timbers to give way at any moment and Fleet and I to be plunged into the green waters below. It was an unpleasant thought because I'd never had a chance to practice swimming in anything deeper than Dancing Creek.

Fortunately, the grey chunks of granite undergirding the walk continued to do their task for a little longer, holding fast despite alarming creaks and groans. A cool breeze blew in off the water, thick with the mingled scents of fish and lakeweed, a combination that soured my stomach this early in the morning. I resisted the urge to cover my nose and focused on my surroundings. It was strangely peaceful here, despite the distant rumble of wagons rolling over the bridges above. The lake lapped gently against the dock's pilings. Gulls clamored in the distance.

I looked across the green expanse and realized for the first time how noisy and cloying the city streets were. The thought of abandoning these open spaces again to enter the stifling city walls at day's end seemed unendurable, but I told myself I didn't need to worry about that yet. I could handle only one problem at a time, and right now my concern lay with finding the priest. But looking around me, I couldn't help thinking this appeared an unlikely place to accomplish that goal.

To my left sprawled an array of decaying and abandoned warehouses that looked like they hadn't seen use in decades. By contrast, a collection of small wooden huts erected at the other end of the wharf teemed with activity. Bits of brightly colored laundry fluttered in the open windows of the little dwellings and tendrils of smoke rose from holes in the thatched roofs. Dozens of men and women, river people I decided by their unique appearance, were mending nets, cleaning fish, and going about their daily routines. I saw a group of men near the water's edge laboring over stacks of timber and coils of rope and decided they were constructing the sturdy rafts they were known for. River children played up and down the long piers, dodging beneath the feet of their elders, chasing one another dangerously across unsteady walkways.

Our arrival attracted a good deal of attention. No one shouted or made any move against us, but it was obvious by the flat, hostile gazes directed our way that our presence was an unwelcome intrusion. I stared back at the strangers just as frankly. Their unfamiliar appearance and clothing was unsettling and vaguely threatening in its strangeness.

The men, with the exception of the little ones, wore their heads shaved bald and kept their faces and chests equally bare. The only clothes they bothered with were loose fitting trousers made of the same fabric as the brightly colored sails of their rafts. But there was no impression of nakedness because their arms, torsos, and occasionally even their faces were so heavily patterned with various colors of ink that in many cases I could hardly see the man beneath the tattoos. Any natural skin visible gleamed a dark bronze from long years spent toiling under the sun.

While I was engrossed in studying these people, Fleet had taken the initiative and was approaching one. This river man was a large fellow at the water's edge who was wrestling with a coil of rope to draw in a line of floating logs from the distant shore. With his frustrated scowl and the tenseness of his muscled back, he didn't have the look of a man I would have chosen to interrupt in the middle of his work. But Fleet had already greeted him. I hung back to see how things would play out, reasoning if the street thief got himself thrown into the lake, someone ought to be standing by to fish him out.

I could see by his exaggerated hand gestures, Fleet was making our situation known to the stranger, but the river man's attention never left his work. Fleet talked uselessly to his back for a few minutes, but when neither this man nor the other laborers alongside him showed any indication they were listening to the babbling city man, Fleet eventually gave up his efforts and returned to me.

"This is a waste of time," he complained. "I'll wager they don't even understand a civilized tongue. We'd get farther asking a dog for directions."

But as we walked away I noted how the big river man glanced back at us with a flicker of something dark in his eyes, and I had the decided feeling he understood much more than he let on. We were more successful in our next attempt. This time, Fleet made his inquiries of a tiny, silver-haired old woman whose quick, beady eyes darted up and down the length of us both, reminding me of a curious little bird. I tried not to look at the sharp bone ornament thrust through her chin.

The old one looked unimpressed with the coppers Fleet flashed at her, but her interest was caught by the bright glass bauble dangling from his ear. In the end, he reluctantly parted with it in exchange for information and, cackling gleefully at her trade, the old woman informed us with gestures and a smattering of the Known tongue what she knew of the man we sought. She told us to ask after him at the home of the woman named Seephinia, out on the water. We took this to mean Seephinia lived among the flotilla of river rafts anchored a short distance from the docks.

Fleet caught a passing river boy and offered him a copper to lead us to this Seephinia. The child didn't need to know our tongue to recognize the coin flashed beneath his nose, and he led us to a small float, constructed of a few flimsy wooden planks lashed across the backs of a pair of barrels and tied at the end of a pier.

Fleet took one doubtful look at the craft and told me, "I've gotten you this far. Surely you can manage the rest on your own."

It was unclear whether it was the water he feared or the possibility of getting his clothes wet. Either way, I seized his arm, even as he was wishing me luck and attempting to back away, and leapt down onto the bobbing raft, hauling him after me in a single rough motion. He'd proven he had a way with these river people, and I wasn't about to plunge myself into their midst alone.

In the end, it wasn't strength that decided the issue, but the precariousness of our position. The raft sank ominously low in the water the moment we clambered on board and all other concerns had to be dismissed in the effort to stay afloat. We quickly shifted ourselves so our weight was evenly distributed across the planks, but my feet were already soaked ankle-deep in water before we pushed off from the dock. I could tell my calf muscles were going to start cramping if I had to stay crouched for long in the awkward position I'd chosen but didn't dare shift my weight. Even the smallest movements sent the raft dipping wildly.

The lake must not have been very deep here because the youth guiding us took up a long, thick stick and poled us forward through the water. He was a skinny boy and when he quickly tired, I took over the task. There were no such offers from Fleet, but I was learning not to expect them. We passed beneath the immense arcing bridge I had crossed into the city only days ago, and seeing it from this angle, I decided the great stone monster looked oddly out of place on the placid lake—a stark contrast to the natural surroundings. It was a relief when we came out from beneath its heavy shadow and I felt the warmth of the sun on my shoulders again.

I didn't really need the boy to guide me because the floating village of the river people was clearly visible from here. As we approached, I studied the string of large rafts bobbing ahead. These were nothing like the smaller working floats navigating back and forth across the lake but were barges long and wide enough to accommodate a handful of little huts on their decks. Where one barge ended, it was lashed to the next with rope bridges or temporary plank walkways spanning the gap over the water. I couldn't help admiring their sturdy, economical construction and appreciating how these temporary dwellings didn't mar the natural landscape, as we land dwellers had done with the stone edifices towering at my back.

I saw brown figures in colorful dress moving on the long decks ahead, hauling in nets of fish and leaping agilely from one barge of their floating village to the next. It looked like most of the river people population lived out on the lake, shunning the shabby hovels built for them on the docks, and I could see why they preferred their barges. Out here, they were free to lift their anchors at any time they pleased and drift away from the city's shadow.

Drawing up to the nearest barge, a long craft that dwarfed our little float, we grated roughly against its timbers as we came to a stop and then our boy was over the side and securing our float to the barge. I didn't realize until I stood on the deck of the larger craft what a relief it was to have my feet on a more or less firm surface, even if that surface was still bobbing gently on the water. Our tiny float had unnerved me with all its lurching and pitching over the waves, and it was obvious the passage had been still harder on Fleet, whose face was drawn into the queasy lines of a man trying valiantly not to lose the contents of his stomach all over his boots. Unfortunately, my friend was granted little time to recover, because our boy was already scurrying off, bare feet slapping across the rough deck as he ran. We had to follow more slowly, since Fleet didn't have his sea legs under him yet and, as the one largely responsible for his being here, I could hardly abandon him.

Our visit attracted the same level of interest here as it had back on the docks. There were many of the bronze-skinned river folk aboard, hauling or mending nets, repairing sails, or completing unfamiliar tasks I couldn't guess at. As we cut a path through them, they dropped their work and turned to stare after us with cold eyes. I had the distinct feeling we might be thrown overboard at any moment, but, as on the docks, no one raised hand or voice to prevent our intrusion.

When we had moved safely beyond the knot of workers, our boy led us to a small hut made of thick shoots of some heavy reed I didn't recognize. Identical to its neighbors, the dwelling was covered by a thatched roof with an open smoke hole in its center and could be entered by means of an open doorway at its front, across which hung a red tarpaulin. I say *could* be entered, because we didn't have the opportunity to proceed that far.

Our young guide approached a small, dark-haired woman sitting cross-legged to one side of the doorway and leaning against the hut. Her nimble fingers were busily stringing muscle shells of all sizes onto a long bit of twine and beside her rested a basket overflowing with still more shells, most of them glistening wetly in the morning sun as if just recently collected from the water. I was immediately struck by her beauty, despite her middling years and the grey streaking the black hair at her temples. Her face and the backs of her hands were patterned with a swirling map of red ink, much like the tattoos of the men back on the docks, and strands of wooden beads and painted shells descended from her earlobes, down to her shoulders, setting off a soft rattling noise whenever she moved her head.

She moved it now, tilting her head back to listen, as our guide rattled off something unintelligible in the river folk tongue. The woman hardly spared a glance in our direction before jabbering back something equally incomprehensible, but I got the impression she was displeased. The youth frowned and lifted his shoulders at her question and she fired off a command that sent him scurrying away. It was all I could do not to grab his shoulder as he ran past and demand he stay. I had no desire to be left alone with the strange, hostile looking woman now setting aside her work to turn her full attention on us. But I reminded myself I still had Fleet to back me up, even if he wasn't, when last I looked, fit for much.

A glance at the street thief now revealed he appeared to be feeling suddenly stronger. He flipped an extra coin to the boy as he darted past, more, I thought, for the eyes of the beautiful river woman than for the sake of his own generosity. His water sickness seemed all but banished as he approached the woman.

"Good day to you, mistress," he said. "My name is Fleet and this is my friend Ilan. I don't know how much the lad explained to you, but we're looking for someone called Seephinia, who we've been told could direct us to a good friend of ours."

I would hardly have categorized Hadrian as a good friend, but I didn't correct the street thief's embellishment. The river woman's blank expression and prolonged silence must have put Fleet off balance because after a long stretch of silence, his polite smile faltered and he flicked me an annoyed glance.

"Told you these people couldn't understand a civilized tongue," he muttered. "Heathens, nothing but heathens."

Slipping his smile back into place, he leaned closer to the river woman. "FRIENDS," he all but bellowed into her ear. "WE SEEK FRIENDS, YES?"

He emphasized this with a few hand gestures I supposed were meant to make things clearer but which made no more sense to me than they probably did to the river woman.

After allowing my companion to make a fool of himself with his shouting for a few moments longer, the river woman turned her cool dark eyes on me.

"I am Seephinia," she said in a heavy accent. "My nephew"—she nodded after the boy—"tells me you seek the Gray Robe. Why this is?" Although her words were slightly jumbled, I understood her well enough.

I had previously given Fleet only the barest explanation of my search for Hadrian, and I had no intention of divulging any more of it to this stranger. "It's a personal matter," I said stiffly. "Just trust me. Hadrian will want to see me." I hoped that was true.

Her eyes narrowed disapprovingly, although I failed to understand what I said to offend her. Was this the casual hostility we attracted from all the river folk or something more personal? It didn't matter. I came for the priest, and I wasn't backing down over a few hard looks. That said, I wasn't going to be foolish about this either.

"Look," I said placatingly. "I've come a long way to see my friend on a matter of importance. I would be very grateful for any help you could offer, and I'm sure the Gray Robe would be appreciative too."

Her expression grew unreadable, but I could feel her considering my words. I could have kicked Fleet when he had to chip in just then with a condescending bribe. "There'll be a shiny copper in it for you as well."

The river woman ignored him and kept her black eyes fixed on me. "I learn the truth—Ilan," she said, with a slight pause before and after my name, as if she was not entirely pleased with the taste of it. "If you are friend to the Gray Robe, I take you to him. If you lie, I cast you to the fish."

"Sounds fair enough." I agreed, my words coming out with more confidence than I felt. "I have nothing to hide."

She sniffed, looking me up and down. "We see," she said.

She rose to her feet in one fluid movement, drawing stares from both Fleet and me. I hadn't noticed until now that she wore only a strip of green cloth wrapped around her from shoulders to thighs. I had never seen a woman walking around in public so scantily clad and, judging by Fleet's expression, he hadn't either. I dug my elbow into his ribs, aware even as I did it that the motion was observed by the river woman and rendered pointless.

She ducked through the covered entrance of the hut and Fleet and I made as if to follow, but she held up a hand, indicating we should wait outside, while she disappeared wordlessly into the darkened interior.

When the canvas closed safely behind her, Fleet gave a low whistle and said, "I've got to tell you, Ilan, I was a little surprised at you just now. I've never seen anyone get a stranger's back up so quick."

"What?" I said, jaw dropping. "You shout in the woman's face like she's an idiot, talk over her head about what an ignorant savage she is, and round it all off by drooling over her bare legs, and you think I'm the one who offended her? If she tosses us overboard it'll be for your bad manners and disgusting leers, not for anything I did."

Fleet sighed and said, "Ilan, Ilan, it's clear you know nothing about what a woman appreciates in a man."

I stared incredulously. "Why, you—I *am*

a woman!"

But he seemed not to hear. "It's obvious you're going to get us both neck deep in trouble if I let you have your way," he said. "So do us a favor, will you? When she comes back, just keep quiet and let me do the talking."

There was no telling what my response would have been, because at that precise moment, the river woman ducked her head out the canvas. I started, torn between wondering how she had returned so quickly and worrying about whether she had overheard our conversation.

Her flat gaze gave nothing away. "The Gray Robe asks for you."

"You mean you've got him inside?" I asked, surprised to learn he could be so near.

Fleet jumped in here. "We deeply appreciate your trouble," he told the frowning river woman. "I apologize for my companion's manners. She doesn't get out of the woods much and isn't accustomed to dealing with people."

She ignored him, instead looking at me, as she firmly blocked the entrance to the hut. "I not see what business you have with the Gray Robe, but if he permits, is not my concern. But I warn you this, drylander. The Gray Robe has many..."—She frowned, as if searching for the right word in our tongue—"...many who wish him hurt..."

"Enemies?" I supplied.

She glared. "If you are one of these, I flay you like a fish and throw your guts into lake."

She sounded perfectly serious.

Beside me, Fleet gave a nervous little laugh, but I took her at her word, having already noted the curved knife tucked into the cord at her waist. I hadn't the slightest doubt she was capable of using it for gutting more than fish. Or at least of attempting to, if she could catch either of us.

I nodded with the most complacent look I could summon, and she stepped aside, allowing us to enter the doorway of the small hut.

"Shouldn't have got her back up," Fleet whispered again, as we crowded through the entrance. I pretended not to hear.

The interior was shaded and after stepping in from the bright sunlight, it took a moment for my eyes to adjust. The space was small and crowded, with cluttered shelves lining the walls and stacks of baskets and large earthenware jars shoved into corners. A mat of woven reeds covered the floor and here and there colorful cushions were scattered around the room. I guessed these to be for seating, since the only true furnishing in the room was a low table set out in the center of the living space. There was another doorway letting out the back of the hut and its leather hanging was tied back, affording a view out over the water. A cool cross breeze swept through the doorways at either end of the room, carrying with it a musical clattering sound, like the soft tinkle of wind chimes. I looked upward and saw the sound came from numerous strings of painted shells and bits of carved wood hanging suspended from the low ceiling.

Hadrian the priest was nowhere in sight. The river woman padded across the room to a curtained alcove partitioned off from the rest of the living space, ducked her head around the divider, and muttered something in her native tongue to someone I couldn't see. I didn't hear the quiet reply, but in a moment the curtain was shoved aside and a broad figure emerged. With a flood of relief, I recognized the priest man.

CHAPTER EIGHT

NOT UNTIL I SAW THE priest did I realize how anxious I had been. It hadn't occurred to me before to wonder what I would do if this were all some trick of the river woman's. But on that score my fears were instantly put to rest, because there was no mistaking the priest, even if his mode of dress was different enough to startle me. Gone were the gray robes, which had always looked incongruous on him anyway, and the chainmail he used to wear beneath. In place of that costume, he now wore a loose cotton shirt and the same wide-legged trousers worn by the river men. His skin had darkened since the last I saw him, I supposed from his days out on the water, so that he could almost pass as one of the river people.

No, at first glance he hardly appeared the warrior priest I sought, and I felt a brief stab of disappointment. If he had set aside generosity as easily as he had shed sword and mail, my efforts to locate him would all have been for nothing. What if he didn't even remember me? Or worse, what if he did, but he no longer held such a charitable view towards woods thieves? Might he betray me to the city guard? My hand moved of its own accord to brush the lightwood of my bow for reassurance before I remembered I couldn't reach the weapon, as it was still covered by my coat.

Luckily, after the briefest of pauses, recognition flickered in Hadrian's eyes.

"Ah, it is the little woods thief who tried to kill me on the road through Dimmingwood," he said.

I was relieved his tone held more amusement than malice.

"Forgive me, but I have to correct your memory," I said. "I believe it was you who threatened to kill me. You were going to cut my throat if my friends didn't meet your demand to free the other travelers."

"So I was. How could I forget? You've grown quite a bit since our last meeting. Upon my mother's ashes, I almost didn't recognize you. I was just wondering the other day whatever became of my ragged, thieving friend. So you finally decided to take up my offer, did you? I have to confess surprise at seeing you here, since I had the impression on our last meeting that you were less than enthralled with me. But I suppose it was inevitable the magic would draw you to me."

"Magic?" This came from Fleet, who leaped into the conversation before I had a chance to respond. "What's this about magic, eh? No one said anything about dark powers to me. Have you been keeping secrets? I haven't been running about all this time with some kind of necromancer, have I?"

His tone was jesting, but I recognized the touch of fear that crept across his face, sensed the hidden revulsion most folk of the province harbored toward those with magical abilities. But Fleet was a professional and his look of unease was swiftly put aside to be replaced with something else. By the scheming glint in his eyes, I knew he was considering how he might use my abilities to his advantage.

I realized I'd better sweep this thing under the rug. If the street thief knew for certain I had the faintest touch of magic in me, he'd be hounding me for the rest of my days to jump into a dozen dishonest schemes he needed my skills to pull off.

"No magic, Fleet," I ground impatiently, casting a warning look at Hadrian. "Just a joke between me and the priest. Now keep quiet. My friend and I haven't seen one another in a bit and we've things to discuss."

Fleet lapsed into disappointed silence.

Hadrian, seemingly oblivious to the danger he had almost plunged us into with his slip, said to me, "I hoped you would come. All things considered, it's for the best."

He must have noticed when I stirred uncomfortably, for he changed the subject. "I should have known it was you on my doorstep by Seephinia's description. But of course, she described a young woman, not the half-grown child I remembered. Then, when she described your companion, a mannerless fellow decked out in baubles like a Camdon lady's maid—well, then I was just confused. I have to say, he doesn't look like one of your forest brothers in roguery."

Fleet, frowning at the unflattering description of himself, flicked a sullen glance up and down Hadrian's person. "This is your friend, Ilan?" he asked. "I thought you wanted an Honored priest, not some fish-eating river rat."

The river woman, who had been hovering in the background, moved closer and there was menace in her eyes and in the way she stroked the hilt of the fish knife tucked into her belt.

I wasn't the only one to notice.

"Hold back, Seephinia," said Hadrian. "The fellow is ill-mannered, but I trust he means no harm."

His eyes contradicted the statement. He wasn't going to ask me again who Fleet was or why I had brought him, but I sensed his curiosity.

The priest looked at me with a raised eyebrow, and I realized he could feel me picking at his emotions. I gritted my teeth. I had become so accustomed to exploring the stream of emotions constantly flowing through the world around me, I'd forgotten I wasn't the only one who possessed that ability.

When I snapped my searching tendrils of magic back into myself, the priest's expression suggested approval, but it bothered me that I now had only his outward expressions to go on. Then I was annoyed at myself. Was I becoming so dependent on my magic these days that I felt crippled when I had to set it aside? Even the bow was taunting me now, I could feel its whispers tickling at the back of my mind, but I didn't dare let them in. Not in the presence of this man.

"This is Fleet," I said suddenly, to cover the awkward lull. "He's a new acquaintance but has already done me a service or two, including helping to find you. He's a little rough around the edges but not a bad sort. I'd be worse than offended if any harm befell him."

I glanced at the river woman as I said that last and she returned my look so flatly I suspected my endorsement had done Fleet more harm than good. She appeared to have even less liking for me than for him and I couldn't figure out why. I'd certainly treated her with a good deal more respect.

Hadrian smiled, the expression a mixture of amusement and mild impatience. At least, that's what I thought it was, but without my magic he was difficult to read.

"I think we'd better start this meeting over," the priest said. "Come, both of you. Sit and make yourselves comfortable. Everyone is welcome here, and I don't keep my guests on their feet." He glanced at the river woman and added, "Nor do I murder them after I've invited them to stay."

As he spoke, he led us to a circle of cushions scattered along the floor. Once we were comfortably settled, Hadrian asked the river woman to fetch us something to drink and when she had gone, Fleet remarked that he had never heard of river folk who would serve drylanders.

Hadrian frowned and said, "Seephinia's no servant but a friend. Her people are too independent to be commanded by any one person. The Praetor may think he has bought them, but the river folk don't see themselves as owned and I think if he or the other drylanders presume otherwise for long, they will discover the truth to their hurt."

Fleet said, "You speak like one of them. Do you forget, Honored, that you're one of us cursed drylanders?"

"I've lived among the river people long enough that I do occasionally forget the ways of my own kind and feel as if I had been born on the water," Hadrian admitted.

I wanted to pursue this subject further, because I was curious to learn what had brought the priest to this spot in the first place. But at that moment Seephinia returned with a steaming, sweet-scented drink. I took one sip from the yellow cup carved of fruit rind that she presented and had no desire for a second.

"It takes getting used to," Hadrian told me with a smile that made me wonder whether my distaste was that obvious or if he was using some trick to read my mind, despite having indicated he disapproved of such uses for magic. I could sense no other presence in my head, but a man as experienced in the magic as he was might know ways to cloud my senses to his delving.

Over drinks, the priest kept the conversation on light pleasantries, asking whether we'd had difficulty finding him here and inquiring about our impressions of the river folk and their floating village. I wondered if this simple talk was to distract me from what he could be doing inside my head and decided I didn't care if it was. Let him dig.

When the small talk began to peter out, I recognized signs of boredom in Fleet's restless fidgeting and so did Hadrian.

"Seephinia," the priest said. "I think our friend would like it if you took him out and showed him the rest of the village. I'm sure he would enjoy a rare glimpse into our daily routines around here."

The river woman scowled but beckoned impatiently for Fleet to follow her. It was clear he was torn between reluctance to put himself in the midst of the "savages" again and a desire to snatch a few moments alone with the attractive Seephinia. I heaved a sigh of relief when his inward struggle ended and he hurried out the curtained doorway after her. I had little doubt I'd be fishing his remains out of the river in half an hour's time, if it took him even that long to provoke her sufficiently, but it was worth it to have the chance to talk with Hadrian alone. We'd been here an hour and I had yet to broach either of the subjects on my mind.

"Interesting fellow, your friend," Hadrian said when they had gone. "He doesn't have the way of the wood folk about him." It still wasn't quite a question.

"He isn't one of the band," I admitted. "I met him only yesterday, when I did him a favor and he agreed to help me find you in return. He's an underhanded sort and I wouldn't turn my back on him, but I can't help liking him."

"He's a thief, of course."

"I can't really say," I returned guardedly.

"You don't have to. He pocketed the spoon from his drink."

"I'll get it back," I promised, my face warming.

"Don't worry about it. It's nothing valuable. I suppose habit took him."

I said curtly, "It doesn't matter whether it's of value or not. I'm the one who brought him here and I'm responsible for what he does in your house. I'll wring his neck when he returns."

"You're growing fairly heated over such a small issue," Hadrian said, regarding me curiously over the rim of his empty cup. "What's really troubling you? Something must be awfully important to have dragged you away from the shadow of your beloved forest. It's the magic, isn't it? It calls to you, the same way it drew me as a youngster. I couldn't rest until I had mastered it and discovered its secrets. From our first meeting I've sensed that same hunger in you."

I stirred uneasily. I had always considered my magic a thing to be used for my own purposes, and I didn't like his talking like it was a living entity compelling me to act. As if I had no choice or say in where it might lead me. I pushed the unpleasant thought aside, telling myself there would be time to examine it later. Right now, this conversation was awakening another, larger concern that had been looming in my mind lately. And for once, it wasn't about Terrac.

"It isn't my magic that's the problem," I told Hadrian, dropping my eyes to the bow, as though it could do my explaining for me. I had removed it and my coat on arrival, and the weapon now stood propped against my knee. It was quiet for the moment, but it wasn't the natural stillness of an inanimate object lacking life of its own. No, there was a spark there. I could sense it as vividly as I had the first time I held the bow in my hands. I felt it was listening to us now. Waiting for something.

Hadrian's gaze followed mine to the bow. "Interesting weapon you've got there," he said. "And those are unusual runes. Mind if I take a closer look?"

At my agreeing, he reached for the bow, saying, "I haven't seen carvings like this since—"

He broke off midsentence as his hands met the pale lightwood. His eyes widened and I couldn't help feeling the shock rolling off him in waves. He was too distracted to hold the feelings in.

Yanking his fingers back as if stung, he said, "Why didn't you warn me this—this thing is alive? And how is that even possible?"

"You tell me," I returned a touch smugly. The priest was a difficult man to shake and ordinarily I would have enjoyed his amazement. That was, if my own mystification hadn't been as great as his.

He observed, "This bow has awareness. It has intentions and emotions, the same as any breathing being."

"Not quiet," I corrected. "Its chief feeling seems to be a lust for violence. I don't think I've ever sensed anything peaceful from it. Mostly, it just hates and longs to drown that hate in blood."

"You knew? You've felt this *life essence* before?"

I shrugged. "The bow and I have had a little time to become acquainted. It's mine, after all. At least, I used to think it belonged to me. Lately, I've begun to feel it goes both ways."

I glared darkly at the object in question.

"Tell me everything," Hadrian said briskly. "Where did you acquire this remarkable object and for how long has it been alive? We'll lay everything on the table and see what sense we can make of it. "

And so I launched into the tale of my discovery of the bow on the night Brig died. Hadrian was a good listener. He heard my story out right up to the point where Terrac and I had burned Brig's body and made our way back to Rideon's camp. We were interrupted at this point in the tale by the return of Fleet and Seephinia. At their entrance, I fell into an awkward silence and Hadrian, apparently seeing my discomfort, dropped the matter and began plying Fleet with small talk. But his eyes promised we would get back to our subject as soon as we were able.

Fleet and I were invited to stay for the noon meal. We accepted and were soon gathered around a low table. Hadrian made for interesting dinner conversation and even Fleet could be witty and amusing in his ridiculous attempts to charm the beautiful river woman. My mind lifted from my troubles and I began to relax. For the first time in a long time I found myself almost content. Then I caught a glimpse of my bow, propped against the near wall, and the sight of it was like a dash of cold water.

CHAPTER NINE

D INNER WAS A SIMPLE AFFAIR. The river woman served us fish with a sort of crusty bread dipped in fruit syrup, and we ate the meal straight off the wooden slabs it was carried in on. During the meal I came to understand it was Seephinia who was our true host and that this hut on the river barge belonged to her. Hadrian was as much a guest as the rest of us, even if he behaved so at home I could almost believe he had been here forever.

The priest explained that he had been staying among the river folk since his arrival in Selbius, in hopes of learning something of their secretive lifestyle. When Fleet asked what he could hope to learn from such people and expressed the opinion Hadrian would do better to teach them our more civilized ways, the priest disagreed and deftly changed the topic. A vague suspicion began to form in my mind, but I let it go for now, promising myself I would discover the truth later. In the meantime, these river people would bear watching. Perhaps they were more than they seemed.

Throughout the meal, Seephinia didn't join

us but stood off to one side, ready to wait on us like the servant Hadrian insisted she wasn't. The priest whispered it had to do with custom. River people had a lengthy set of rules by which they lived their lives and a great part of these centered around particular behaviors toward guests. The promise of hospitality was not easily achieved by strangers, but once it was attained, a visitor could be assured of receiving every comfort and respect.

Despite this reassuring information, the river woman continued to fix me with a cold eye. I remained at a loss as to what I had done to deserve such hostility but shrugged it off. As long as she didn't poison my fish, she could dislike me all she wanted. And at least her disapproval was limited to me and, to a lesser extent, Fleet. For Hadrian she clearly had a great admiration.

Conversation during dinner finally came around to Terrac. I nearly choked on my sweetbread when Fleet brought up the subject, for my thoughts had become so preoccupied with the bow I'd almost allowed myself to lose sight of the more urgent matter. I spilled out the story now of the Fist's ambush and Terrac's capture, ending with his condition the last time I laid eyes on him, as I was forced to leave him in the hands of the Praetor's men. Hadrian heard me out and I finished my tale with a plea that he aid me in discovering the fate of my friend. Assuming Terrac was still alive, I would need help in bringing him out of captivity.

Asking the priest for help didn't grate on my

pride as it once would have. I seemed to be growing accustomed to begging.

By the time my tale was over and I fell silent, my throat was hoarse from too much speaking. I had no idea how much time had passed, but, during it, the meal had been consumed and Seephinia had disappeared, carrying off the remains of our repast. Flies were droning over the drips of syrup that had been spilled across the tabletop. Fleet, who had already heard my story, displayed little interest in the retelling and was leaning back from the table looking bored and mildly sulky. The latter was, I supposed, due to the river woman's departure.

Hadrian looked thoughtful, gazing into the depths of the mug in his hands, and while I awaited his response, I agonized over second thoughts. Had I been mistaken to reveal so much of my plans him? Just because he had once offered to tutor me in magic didn't mean he wanted to become entangled in illegal activities. After all, he was a priest of the Light and, beyond that, an honest man.

I looked up from the tabletop to find his eyes on me. "So..." he said slowly, and the word hung in the air until I felt like squirming. "You are asking me to aid you in plucking an arrested criminal from the grip of justice?"

"No," I said. "It isn't as it sounds. I know what you think of the band, and I wouldn't ask you to become involved in anything to do with Rideon or the rest. But you must believe me when I say Terrac isn't one of us. Not really. He's just an innocent boy who would be a priest had he not somehow gotten swept up in things that weren't his concern."

Hadrian appeared not to hear. He said stiffly, "I think you have misunderstood my previous offer to help. I believed you were here for instruction and perhaps council on a difficult point."

I grimaced, but he didn't speak of magic or the bow.

"However," he continued, "it now seems that wasn't your intention. So let me make this very clear—to both of you." His gaze swung to encompass Fleet as well. "I want nothing to do with any of your dishonest activities. My offer to instruct you, Ilan, was as simple as it sounded. I never meant to suggest I would aid you in endeavors stretching beyond the bounds of the law. I trust we now understand one another."

He leaned back, removing his hands from the tabletop and his voice became suddenly brisk. "I had thought to invite the pair of you to stay for a few days, but I think now it would be for the best if you both left right away."

I was halfway to my feet before he'd finished speaking.

"Come, Fleet," I commanded. "I thought we might find a champion of justice here, but I see I made a misjudgment."

I bowed formally to the priest, not caring that the gesture came off clumsy for my having never tried it before.

"My mistake, Honored One," I said. "I'm sorry to have wasted your time and mine—and more importantly, Terrac's, for I'm sure he has little of it left. I bid you good day."

I was all eagerness to be gone from the place. It was suddenly unspeakably galling that I had accepted this man's hospitality and eaten bread at his table, food for which I had no way to pay him. The restricting confines of common decency forbade even planting a knife through his ribs on my way out the door. But I was most furious of all with myself for having let down my guard long enough to trust this comparative stranger in the first place.

I strode to the doorway and although I heard Fleet nearly upsetting the table in his haste to scurry after me, I didn't slow for him. We were nearly out when I recalled I had left my bow behind and was forced to make an undignified about-face to march back for it, detracting heavily from the dramatic exit I had in mind.

As I grabbed the bow, Hadrian cut into my furious thoughts. "You can leave as angry as you please. But I'll ask you not to insult me as you go by spouting sanctimonious lies about championing justice. I believe I know a thing or two on the subject, having been a Blade of that order before you were born."

"Were you even listening to a word I said?" I asked. "My friend is innocent. He's been mistakenly assumed guilty of crimes he never committed and is in danger of suffering a punishment he doesn't deserve—if he hasn't already. If that doesn't constitute a miscarriage of justice, I don't know what does."

The stress of the past days came rushing in on me and my anger gave way to despair, so I stopped short of the insults I was about to shout in the priest's face. Instead, I sighed, scrubbed a weary hand across my face, and said, "But maybe I'm wrong. Maybe you have the right of it and I should just stand back and allow my friend to suffer while I escape and live free for another day. What makes Terrac's fate my responsibility? He had just as much chance to escape as I." *Except that he had come after me that day to say farewell.* If not for me, he would never have run into the Fists. That made all the difference.

"You truly believe in this boy's innocence," Hadrian said quietly. "You care about him."

"Yes."

"And you seek no gain for yourself?"

"None," I said.

"That is very un-scoundrelish of you. In fact, you're in danger of doing a thing some would call noble," he said.

"I'm glad you find that amusing. But what am I standing here for?"

I would have turned away but suddenly Hadrian was blocking my path.

"Don't be so hasty," he said. "Put away your bow, sit down, and we'll talk things over carefully.

This time, I promise to reserve judgment."

As he spoke, he moved to take the bow from my hands. I tightened my grip, surprised at the flare of possessiveness I felt at another person attempting to handle the weapon.

Hadrian noticed and dropped his voice so that not even Fleet could hear. "I'm not forgetting there are other things we need to talk about as well," he said quietly.

CHAPTER TEN

W E SPENT THE REMAINDER OF the daylight hours and sat up late into the night discussing Terrac's situation and what should be done about it. It didn't take me long to realize enlisting the aid of the priest may have been a mistake. At this point, it appeared Hadrian might do our cause more harm than good. Once I had convinced him Terrac's worst crime was to become involved with the wrong people, he was nearly as determined as I to see him spared a wrongful fate. Unfortunately, his ideas on how to go about the rescue were a little more legal than anything I had in mind. He wanted to meet with the Praetor, have Terrac brought forward for a chance to defend himself, and bring me out to shed light on the truth.

He seemed oblivious to the fact the only witness to the boy's innocence was a bedraggled woods thief who, the moment she admitted her association with the band of Rideon the Red Hand, would be clapped in irons herself. I wanted to save Terrac all right but not at the cost of *my* neck. For that matter, I wouldn't endanger the band either and it was certain I would be doing so if I complied with Hadrian's plan. Maybe in the world Hadrian liked to imagine, the authorities would gratefully accept the testimony of an admitted outlaw and allow me walk free. But this wasn't that place. The nearest authority in the region was the Praetor, a man not known for his tolerance of outlaws, particularly those associated with the Red Hand. I didn't want to imagine what Rideon's reaction would be if he knew I was even contemplating such an action.

Fleet promoted an altogether different approach. I should storm the dungeons and slaughter the guards, rescue Terrac, and carry him back to the safety of Dimmingwood. Or, even more brilliant, I could force my way into the keep at the heart of the city, murder any opposition, and take the very Praetor prisoner, holding him on threat of death until he ordered my friend freed. I would be carrying all this out alone, of course, because Fleet would have no involvement with either plan, despite both having been his idea.

What none of us wanted to mention was the possibility all our planning could prove to be for nothing. We couldn't be certain Terrac was even alive, considering the last time I saw him he'd had an arrow in his back.

We finally decided our first action must be to learn exactly what had befallen him since then and, once his position was known, we could build our plans from there. Here our consensus ended, because no one could put forth a reasonable suggestion on how this information should be attained. The priest and the street thief were at odds on every possibility, and as the night drew on, I developed a splitting headache from listening to their bickering. The candles the river woman lit around the room had burned low and still Fleet and Hadrian worried at one another's plans like a pair of dogs at opposite ends of a bone. Seephinia had long since retired.

My eyelids drooped, the voices of my companions growing distant, as the failing light carved deep shadows across their faces. I leaned my head against the wall, sleep crept in to claim me, and I slipped blissfully into a place where cool forest shadows enveloped me and the only sounds were the singing of crickets and the familiar rustling of leaves and creaking treetops swaying overhead.

The next three days found the situation scarcely changed. I eventually talked Hadrian out of his foolish plan and together we persuaded Fleet to see the flaws in his schemes as well. We decided Fleet would spend the days hanging around the taverns in Selbius, picking up gossip from off-duty city guardsmen frequenting those places, as well as pursuing information from his less reputable connections in the city. He didn't speak of it, but I knew he was also checking the pillories in the market square daily and that he made it a regular practice to walk past the east bridge in the common district, where executions routinely took place.

We were living in uneasy times, and the Praetor believed the only hope of curbing the rising lawlessness of the province lay in taking swift and decisive measures against crime. Light pickpockets were strung up alongside violent criminals with little distinction between the two and, from what I heard, on little more evidence than rumor or a doubtful witness or two standing up at a mock trial. The more I considered these things, the more the fear grew within me that I had arrived too late for Terrac.

Hadrian did his part. Having made it clear from the beginning he had no intention of going through illegal channels to restore Terrac to freedom, he nonetheless set about the endeavor in his own way with a will. Like Fleet, he put the word out among a number of friends in the city, ones he trusted to be discreet, that certain parties would be interested to know of the condition and exact whereabouts of a priest boy named Terrac, suspected to be under the custody of the Praetor's Fists. He also enlisted the help of Seephinia and a small number of others in the river folk community. I don't know how he persuaded them to take an interest in our affairs, because they usually bore nothing but contempt for drylanders. But they nurtured an inexplicable respect for Hadrian and at his request agreed to brave the noise and confines of the city, where they kept their eyes and ears open for news of Terrac.

What was I doing while the others were working

so industriously to save my friend? As it turned out, I was the only member of our little conspiracy remaining idle through those long days. Hadrian felt it would be the wisest course to keep me on the river rafts and away from the city as much as possible. I had an air about me, he said, which screamed woods folk and as these were regarded with a measure of suspicion by the city dwellers, it might be best not to call unwanted attention on ourselves by waving me like a flag beneath the noses of the city guard.

I protested, of course. I had more right to be involved than anybody, and I was no more a risk than Fleet, who couldn't resist slipping his hand into the pocket of every fifth passerby on the streets. But my protests did me no good. Hadrian said Fleet had that skill only street thieves possessed of pulling off his business effortlessly and blending into the milling crowd before anyone took note of him. He knew the backstreets and allies of the city as well as he knew his own dear mother's face, whereas I would only blunder around, slowing him down and attracting attention to his actions.

I couldn't argue with that, no matter how I wanted to.

And so, this was how I came to find myself living in the tiny hut, a semi-permanent guest on a river folk barge. Life carried on somewhat monotonously for me during that time. I suffered moments of sickening anxiety on the occasions when Fleet visited to report his lack of progress, but between these times stretched long hours of boredom, as I found myself trapped on a not particularly large vessel with a handful of strangers, most of whom didn't speak my language.

Seephinia could speak the Known tongue when she was of a mind to, but most of the time she was not. Her initial dislike for me hadn't faded and she showed no inclination toward friendship. At least I had that part cleared up now. It hadn't taken me long to realize the hostility she harbored toward me was the result of my acquaintance with Hadrian. She was as jealous as a hawk over his dinner.

But she had nothing to worry about there. My friendship with the priest was so new I hesitated to call it even that, yet how could I call a man who was risking everything by mere association with me less than a friend? One thing was certain. It was no good making denials to the river woman. She had already made up her mind about me, and in all honesty I almost enjoyed her jealousy. From the beginning, she hadn't been especially pleasant toward me and if I found the occasional opportunity to drag the priest off alone and leave her to sweat a little, I did.

Such opportunities weren't hard to come by because Hadrian and I had much to talk about. One afternoon we talked of the bow. It was a chilly day. We were well into autumn and already a bite could be felt in the wind off the water, offering a foretaste of the winter to come. Back in Dimming, the trees would be stripped mostly bare this late in the season and the forest floor would be littered with dry leaves. I wished I were home to see it.

Hadrian and the river woman had gone out fishing, leaving me alone to pace and worry because Fleet hadn't come to update me on his efforts for over a day now. I didn't know if he had bad news and feared to tell me, if he had been taken up by the city guard and hauled off to prison himself, or if he was just having too good a time in his taverns and had forgotten all about me sitting here anxiously awaiting news. I made up my mind to punch him in the head whenever he did decide to come back and sat down to watch the door with that very intention in mind.

This was the state of mind Hadrian found me in when he returned some time later. A more cautious man might've taken a look at my face and found an excuse to turn around and leave, but Hadrian wasn't easily intimidated. If he even noticed my dark scowl, he pretended not to. His attention was immediately drawn to one thing and, as was often the case with him, it was the thing I least wanted him to notice.

"You keep that object close these days, don't you?" he asked.

I knew what he referred to. My bow was propped against my knee, not because I was intending to use it, but because I felt anxious lately when it wasn't near.

"Just the force of habit," I said. "When you were a Blade of Justice you must have slept with your sword in your hand. You never know when you'll need it."

It sounded better than the truth, that I had developed an unreasonable fear my bow would be stolen if I let it out of reach.

"That's different, we were in constant danger in those days, whereas you're safe here. Who do you think you need to defend against? Seephinia? The river people? Or maybe you just don't trust me?"

His intent look made me uncomfortable.

"Mind if I take another look at this peculiar weapon?" he asked abruptly.

Before I could refuse, as he must have known I would, he took the bow from me. Having it plucked out of my hands and seeing it in those of another produced a sharp, unexpected ache inside me and it was all I could do not to snatch it back immediately. But I resisted the impulse and, feeling like an anxious mother wolf watching her pup being sniffed over by a stranger, allowed Hadrian to examine the weapon. He handled it with great care, tracing his fingers along the carvings on the golden-hued wood and remarking on the workmanship. I was pleased he appreciated its uniqueness even as I worried he might admire it too much and decide he wanted it.

"This weapon is a fascinating puzzle," he told me. "The arms are smooth and unworn by handling, as if it were created only yesterday. Even the color of the wood is fresh and new. Yet when I hold it, I sense great age and could almost believe the thing is ancient. And these runes confuse me. I originally thought they were in the old tongue, but now that I look closer, I see they're Skeltai, the tongue of your ancestors and their descendants across the border. Yes, it's definitely Skeltai, but a very old dialect, which I don't think many could interpret today."

"But you can?" I asked eagerly.

He smiled. "You are very interested."

"I've often tried to guess what they say," I admitted.

"Then we're fortunate I was obsessed with ancient dialects when young and spent years amassing such impractical knowledge," Hadrian said. "These differ from what I know of the ancient Skeltai alphabet, but there's enough similarity I can decipher most and take an educated guess at what I don't recognize."

He traced a finger along the runes as he read aloud. "*Power of death my master hath, let fly my arrows and loose my wrath.*"

He looked up, frowning. "That's a rough translation, but Skeltai is so different from our language it's difficult to pin down any closer. There's a little more here, a short bit before and after what I read." He indicated the lines with his thumbnail. "But I'm a little rusty at this and would need to dig out my old books to make sense of the rest."

He changed the subject unexpectedly. "I don't feel comfortable holding this object," he said.

"It doesn't trust me. Perhaps you'd better take it back."

I snatched it from him, hiding my relief at having it safe in my hands again. It seemed to me the bow preferred to be in my keeping. Maybe I had been unjust when I used to think it a cruel object, incapable of any but dark emotion. It felt peaceful enough now.

Hadrian was speaking and it took me a moment to withdraw my mind from the bow and focus on what he said.

"I don't think there can be any doubt it's a magical artifact," he was saying. "The Skeltai are adept at contriving complicated enchantments and hiding them within everyday objects. I don't claim to understand such things, but a mage might know more."

"I thought you were a mage."

"Me, a mage? Never, my young friend. I realize you've been left ignorant on subjects relating to magic, but surely even you know the difference between Natural and Trained magic."

The look on my face must have spoken volumes, for he sighed and smiled a little. "I can see the time has come for a little elementary lesson. Let us set aside your mysterious bow for a while and talk magic."

He took the bow from me and put it off to one side, shaking his head when I would have tried to take it back.

"Leave it, Ilan," he said. "It will be there when

we've finished, and I think our lesson will progress better without it. Its very nature is in opposition to what I want to teach you."

Curiosity held me in check. "Is this the instruction you promised?"

"I don't see when there will be a better time for it, do you?" he asked.

"I suppose not."

"Well then," he said. "To begin with, there are two distinctly different types of magic. It will be best if you separate them in your mind right away. The first is Natural magic, the kind some men and women have from the moment they are born and from which they could no more detach themselves than they could cast aside their own limbs. You and I, we have that magic and both of us have a particular aptitude in the area of life force and emotion. We can sense them in others around us—can even seek them out if we choose. Not all Naturals excel in these areas, but they're the abilities I can teach you the most about because they are the ones we share. It's easier for a fish to teach a fish to swim."

"You said there were two kinds of magic," I reminded him.

"The other kind is the Trained art of the mage," he said shortly. "Trained magic is wrong and dangerous and that's all you need to know about it."

He had lost all traces of his usual good humor, his expression and tone leaving no doubt of his feelings on the subject, even if his words had.

"Seems to me I need to know something about a thing, if I'm to know how to avoid it," I pointed out, rather slyly, I thought.

Hadrian sighed, a defeated sound that neither agreed with nor condemned my suggestion.

He explained, "Mages use a man-developed form of magic that allows those not born with the gift, those never meant to possess it, to bend it to their will nonetheless. This includes the use of incantations, potions, and the endowing of certain objects with magical powers. It's what makes me uncomfortable with your bow. As an enchanted object, it's fascinating, and yet we must never forget it was born of dark magic and may be tainted by the purpose of its makers. Such a weapon could only have achieved its life by the enchantment of one knowledgeable in the arts of the arcane. And one of the few things we know of the Skeltai people is that they are highly possessed of both forms of magic. This is probably why so many of their descendants on this side of the border are born with magical talent. You, for example, may have received more than your silver hair from your Skeltai ancestors."

I focused on the bow, asking, "If it was made by Skeltai, how did it come to be here?"

Hadrian shrugged. "Possibly, we'll never know. But I consider it unfortunate you and that bow ever crossed paths. I have an unpleasant feeling about it."

"You mean because it was enchanted by a mage?" I asked.

Hadrian winced. "I think we've spoken enough of the Trained magic. It isn't a subject any Natural feels at ease with."

"It doesn't bother me," I said. "Incantations and spells all sound very interesting. What exactly can you do with Trained magic that you can't do with the Natural, anyway? Is it stronger?"

Hadrian scowled. "Neither is greater in strength, but the Natural talent is our birthright and the Trained skills are a foul distortion of what ought to be. There is no question which power is best and which is to be loathed."

"Very much loathed," I agreed, although I couldn't see what he was getting so fired up about. "But of this unspeakably evil form of magic, what would you say might be its advantages?"

Maybe he caught a sense of my intent or maybe he just didn't like this line of questioning, because he said firmly, "You will never dabble in the Trained arts, Ilan."

"Never," I agreed soothingly.

He appeared not to have heard. "If I should ever discover you doing anything of the kind..." His voice trailed off ominously and he took a long breath as if to get a grip on his emotions.

"I will not instruct you in such things," he then continued, more calmly. "You would be hard pressed to find anyone who will. Even so, I'll require one thing from you before my tutorage progresses any farther. I've no mind to teach you in the ways of magic, merely to see you use it for selfish purposes, and I don't like to imagine the amount of power that could come of a corrupt blending of the two forms of magic. That kind of strength should not belong to any one person."

His words quickened my heartbeat, but not in the way he doubtless intended. The word "power" kept ringing in my ears until it seemed it had imprinted itself on my brain. A familiar presence nearby echoed my excitement and with one hand I reached out absently to stroke my bow.

Hadrian was still speaking. "The price required in exchange for my instruction is this. You will give me your oath never to delve into any form of magic beyond the bounds of your Natural talent."

I tensed when he spoke of price but relaxed now. I had no money, but an oath I could handle.

"Very well," I said. "I give my word on it, as an outlaw of the band of the Red Hand."

Hadrian's mouth turned up at my relief. "Your word as an outlaw means very little to me, my young friend, and swearing on the honor of that scoundrel Rideon means even less. I want you to swear by something precious to you. Swear by Brig, that outlaw you were so fond of, and I will believe you then."

He had me there. My mouth tightened and I heard how strained my voice came out, but I spoke loudly. "I swear on the memory of Brig that I'll never explore any area of magic not first approved by you."

He looked satisfied with that. His gaze became sympathetic. "I know it was painful for you to have your old friend brought up like that," he said apologetically. "But it is for the best, for now I can trust you wholeheartedly."

He stood and briskly changed the subject. "I think we've had enough of a lesson for one day. How would you like to come out and learn how the river folk load the stone from the quarry to ferry to the island? We'll take a raft out to the lakeshore and maybe lend them a hand. What do you say?"

I followed willingly enough, but my thoughts were occupied elsewhere, and I spent the remainder of the day trying to figure out a loophole around my oath.

CHAPTER ELEVEN

⟶◆◇◆⟵

THE FOLLOWING MORNING I AWOKE to find Hadrian missing. He had left no message, at least none that Seephinia woman would relate to me, and had said nothing of going anyplace the night before. Still, I told myself as I stepped out of the hut, there was nothing to worry about. I was confident that, unlike the still unaccounted for Fleet, the priest was fully capable of avoiding trouble.

As if my thoughts had conjured him up, I found the street thief out behind the hut, soaking his feet in the lake. He told me he had already exchanged words with Hadrian, who had left at the dawn on a mysterious mission ashore, leaving no word of when he meant to return. Fleet thought it likely to be a while.

I fumed at the news. How would we ever find Terrac if everyone kept running off on personal errands? That reminded me of Fleet's laxness of the day before, and I set about taking a full report of his activities now. As is turned out, his findings were nonexistent, unless you counted as progress a purse of purloined coins and a jade ring he had lifted straight from a merchant's finger.

Disgusted, I went back inside, where I consumed a peculiar looking purple fruit I found set out on the table. I took a few gulps of lake water to wash down the stickiness, trying to ignore the brownish tint the water took on after sitting in a pitcher overnight.

Then, to make use of the free time I had on my hands, I stripped down and bathed myself off one side of the barge. It wasn't easy finding a secluded spot for this and in the end, I had to settle for a very partial sort of privacy. But the effort was worth it, because when I pulled myself back onto the deck, the lake water running off me had a decidedly murky cast. Of course the lake hadn't been so clean even before I crawled into it, despite its emerald appearance.

I dressed hastily, not caring that my skin was still damp as I pulled my clothes on. It wasn't really that I expected Hadrian to return while I was occupied, but a spirit of expectancy hung over me that morning. I felt some development in our efforts must take place very soon. Besides, dark clouds had gathered from nowhere to blot out the warm sun, and I clearly didn't have much time left to get inside before the clouds opened up.

I collected Fleet, whom I had posted as a not particularly trustworthy lookout, and together we returned to the shelter of the hut. Within the hour, a downpour began and the wild gale churned the usually calm waters of the lake until our barge was bobbing on the choppy surface. Cold drafts found their way through the cracks between the reeds making up our little shelter, and the howling wind whipped at the canvas sheets over the doorways until I tied them down.

We made an uncomfortable little gathering. Even Seephinia wouldn't go out to work on the floats in such a storm but remained inside with us, mending a heap of stinking fish nets and stringing up more of the little shell ornaments she often sold on the docks. Her presence contributed to the tension of the atmosphere, for she didn't like me and I didn't like her, and Fleet did like her, but she disdained him, and so it was an unpleasant situation all around. I was relieved when she finally disappeared behind that curtained off partition of the hut and didn't emerge again.

Even then, matters were not greatly improved. Poor Fleet soon succumbed to his old water sickness, brought about by the unsteady motion of the heaving barge, and he turned out to be an irritable companion when suffering. Naturally, he couldn't leave the barge in this weather and so took over my sleeping cot.

Left to myself, I snooped around the hut, examining the jars and baskets and whatnots on the shelves along the walls as I could not when Hadrian and the river woman were watching. I found nothing of interest and my curiosity soon wore out, replaced by a returning impatience. Where was Hadrian? It was intolerable that he was out roaming free in the city while I was stuck in this drafty little hut on the lake. My impatience to be on with the task of finding Terrac weighed on me more heavily than ever that afternoon.

Eventually, I reined in my pacing and forced myself to settle down just inside the doorway, where I kept an eye on the worsening storm and sharpened my knives on a whetstone I discovered on one of the shelves. With the sense of urgency hanging over me today, I felt I would need them soon.

Hadrian never returned all that day. Seephinia eventually left her curtained alcove to light the lanterns, as the interior of the hut grew dark. She and I shared an uncomfortable meal of chowder and seacakes, which the afflicted Fleet couldn't be persuaded to share in. The meal was a silent affair and when it was over, the evening stretched long before us.

Night fell and still there was no sign of the priest. This was to be expected, as it would have been foolish for him to attempt crossing the lake in this storm. It would be far wiser to remain in the city and pass the night in an inn. No, there was no call to worry about Hadrian. But I did anyway, up until the hour I finally followed Fleet's example and went to bed. I sensed the river woman wished to be left alone in her vigil.

The first thing I became aware of on waking the

following morning was Hadrian's presence. The priest had returned. He slept through half the morning, and Seephinia wouldn't allow him to be disturbed until he was ready to wake on his own. Frustrated, I went out on the deck where I sat and watched a lot of river children, who were splashing and wrestling with a ball that was somehow made to float atop the water. If there were particular rules to their game I couldn't discern them.

A feeling of premonition was still on me. I couldn't say whether it was my magic or a more basic, human intuition that alerted me to events to come. Whatever it was, it made me anxious, and I felt it was connected to Hadrian.

I was relieved when he shortly sought me out, for I had horrible visions of this day being as long and drawn out as the last. In the harsh morning light, Hadrian looked older, his face haggard, his eyes red-rimmed as if he hadn't slept much the night before. When he sat down beside me, I caught a strong whiff of what on anyone but a priest I would have thought were ale fumes. He wore his gray robes today, the first I had seen of them in a long time, and he slicked his usually wild hair into a tidy tail down the back of his neck. Before sinking down next to me, he had to rearrange his sword, which he wore belted at his hip once more. All these changes signaled something to come, but I didn't know what.

"Good morning, Ilan," he greeted me.

"Priest." I struggled to hold in the questions

that wanted to pour out of me, and by the way one side of his mouth twitched, he knew it.

"I can feel that something happened the other day in the city," I said. "You're entirely too pleased with yourself not to have succeeded. Well, I don't plan to drag the news out of you one piece at time, so spill it."

"You grow more confident every day," he said. "There are instances where that's a good thing, but when it comes to magic, it almost never is. Overconfidence is one the greatest dangers a magicker can face."

"Hadrian," I warned.

"Very well, no lessons today," he conceded. "You want information and here it is. I spent most of yesterday and the entirety of last night in a wretched smoke-filled tavern in the lowest portion of the common district, playing dice with a retired knight of my order, a few strangers of no consequence, and who else was there? Ah yes, a lieutenant of the Praetor's Iron Fists."

"A Fist!" I said. "What did you learn from him? Did you ask about Terrac?"

Hadrian snorted and said dryly, "Your subtlety does you credit. One hardly comes out and asks one of the Praetor's men if he's apprehended any good criminals lately."

"So did you learn anything or didn't you?" I demanded.

"I learned never to buy drinks for a Fist again. They consume more than any three horses. Also, that old comrades in arms, even former Blades of Justice, cheat at dice like anyone else. Next time I'll lure them into a game of sticks and stones to make up my losses."

At my aggravated sigh, he gave way. "All right then, cultivate a little patience, child," he said. "It took me the better part of the night, combined with the contrived loss of a great deal of coin to keep the lieutenant at the table, but I eventually worked the conversation around to related topics. It was a blind shot that if I shook the dice cup something good would come out, but luck was with us this time. The lieutenant spoke of a circumstance that had arisen lately, involving the capture of a young man believed to be a follower of that notorious brigand Rideon the Red Hand."

He hesitated and I wondered how bad the news must be if he was reluctant to relate it. Remembering he was probably aware of my feelings through his magic, I tried to pull my shaken emotions more tightly into myself.

"Go on," I said, my words coming out steadier than I expected. "Just tell me if Terrac lives. Yes or no."

"He lives."

"But?" I prompted.

"But nothing," Hadrian said. "He has been fairly treated from all I heard and seems to be sound of health and limb. There was no mention of his suffering any injury. Are you certain he was shot with an arrow?"

"I saw the wound with my own eyes," I said distractedly, a million questions rushing through my mind. "You say he's well treated. Where is he kept?" I asked. "There must be a way to get a message to him. I have to let him know help is on the way so he doesn't give up hope."

"Are you so certain he wishes to be rescued?"

I shoved the ridiculous question aside. "Who ever heard of a prisoner who wants to stay in captivity? Of course he longs for rescue. What, do you think I'm going to leave him in the cruel hands of those odious Fists forever?"

I returned my thoughts to scheming. "We need to make the rescue soon," I said. "Just because they have taken it into their heads to treat him well today doesn't mean they'll be feeling so generous tomorrow. How soon can I get in touch with him?"

Hadrian shrugged. "You can see him today if you wish. Fleet and I will take you into the city, but we'll disguise you first. You shouldn't go wondering the streets in the garb of a woods villager."

I was startled. "See him today? You mean I can visit him in person? How have you arranged this?" My mind leapt from one conclusion to the next. "You've bribed the Fist lieutenant! No, you've befriended a prison guard!"

"Nothing so dramatic, I'm afraid. Come now. We will send Fleet ashore to procure you some kind of ordinary feminine attire. I don't wish to know how he'll go about it. Then the three of us can be on our way."

Midmorning saw us abandoning the river barge and crossing to the docks on a small raft Hadrian had procured for the purpose. The day was a fine one, the sun warm and the lake calm. The only sign of yesterday's storm was a scattering of debris bobbing near the docks, and that was swiftly being cleaned up by a handful of river men.

It would have been a pleasant crossing if I hadn't been in a state of agitation. I told myself most of my concern was for Terrac and his uncertain situation but had to admit that wasn't the whole of it. Hadrian had insisted I leave my bow behind, and I was uneasy with the separation. Suppose it was stolen while I was out? Or what if Seephinia decided to throw it into the lake, or worse, use it for kindling? I had no doubt she would delight in such an act if she guessed how deeply it would affect me.

And as if all that wasn't enough to worry about, I was having trouble adjusting to the new clothing Fleet had supplied me. I couldn't remember the last time I wore a skirt, and I was finding it impossible to move in this one without tangling the long hem awkwardly around my ankles. I didn't want to imagine how I would swim for shore in such an outfit, if our raft were to tip over.

Luckily, it didn't, and we reached the docks safe and dry. Once we'd left the wharf behind and entered the walls of Selbius, the oppressive crowds and the smothering smells and noises flooded in on all sides. I hadn't set foot in the city in months and had forgotten how high the walls towered and how uncomfortable it was to feel so many people pressing in on every side. It reminded me of the time Terrac and I had explored the caves of Boulder's Cradle back in Dimming and I had gotten wedged tight inside one of the tunnels. I had been trapped so close between the rock walls I could scarcely breathe, and it hadn't taken me long to panic. Fortunately, Terrac kept a cool head and, in one of the few instances where I could remember him ever doing anything useful, had squeezed his slimmer frame into the tunnels to help me work my way loose. The feeling I experienced now was akin to what I'd known then. There was no frantic, mindless terror this time, but the same helpless sense of being stuck tight in these streaming crowds, with little room to maneuver.

Hadrian led us down a main thoroughfare through the heart of the city, until we came to a place where traffic stopped entirely. Here, a large gathering of people clogged the way, as if waiting for something. There was a sense of excitement and anticipation in the air, and I had the feeling Hadrian had brought me here for a purpose. I looked through the sea of strange faces, trying to figure out what I was meant to see, and when I turned back, the crowd had shifted, blocking my companions from view.

Fear set in at once. Only Hadrian knew where

Terrac was. I couldn't lose him. I shoved my way through the press, heedless of the feet I trampled and the offended looks I earned, hoping to glimpse at any second the gray of Hadrian's robes or the flash of blue that was Fleet's coat. Then I saw it, just ahead. With a sigh of relief, I grabbed a blue-clad elbow, but the face turned toward me in the next instant was that of a confused stranger. Releasing the man's arm with a quick apology, I pushed on again in search of the real Fleet.

Something was changing around me. The crowd began to shift, pulling back to the sides of the street, and I found myself carried along with them. I caught a glimpse of several men in the uniform of the city guard and realized it was they who were shoving the crowds back to line the way. A murmur swept the multitude, growing louder until it erupted into indistinct shouts, and the gathering surged forward as one body to press against the barrier formed by the city guards. They were held back, but not roughly, as they strained forward like curious children hoping for a peek at a forbidden sight.

I shouted Hadrian and Fleet's names into the press but was drowned out by the noise. What had the people so excited? A sort of procession was passing down the street, but so many heads blocked my view it was impossible to make out what it was. A parade, perhaps?

Catching sight of a mounting-block in front of the stable of an inn, I thought it would afford me a view over the crowd. I forced my way though the throng, turning a deaf ear to the curses of those I jostled, reached the block, and clambered up. I was a short distance back from the street now, but at least I had a clear view. My stomach lurched as I saw the procession was flanked by the ebony and scarlet of the Praetor's private guard. I'd had too many unpleasant encounters with the Fists lately to look on those colors without a flinch, but I told myself it wasn't fear, but anger that set my heart thundering against my ribs. My hands itched for the feel of my bow. Whatever had possessed me to leave it behind?

I smothered my initial instinct to leap down from the block and put this place behind me. I was hidden in the crowd. There was no reason why anyone should notice me. So I kept still and watched the passing procession. It appeared the Fists were functioning as bodyguards today, accompanying a host of noblemen and ladies. Judging by the hunting gear and the dogs dashing around the horses' hooves, this was a hunting party, returning from the inland to the Praetor's keep.

I observed the finery of the elite class of Selbius society with interest. The ladies wore heavily embroidered dresses with flowing skirts, even while riding, and ankle boots that looked too soft for much walking. The men wore fashionably cut silks and velvets under cloaks so long they trailed down the hindquarters of their mounts. Many sported the same thin triangle of hair on their chins that Fleet wore and this, combined with their vain expressions, reminded me so much of the street thief I could have laughed.

But the urge to do so evaporated as a fluttering motion drew my eyes to a pennant held aloft at the fore of the procession. The emblem of a black bear against a field of scarlet belonged to the house of Tarius, as did the FIDELITY and SERVICE motto beneath. I'd read those words many times on my mother's brooch, but encountering them here so unexpectedly was startling. And when my gaze dropped from the pennant to the man riding beneath, I felt as if I had been doused with cold water.

He was no stranger to me, this middle-aged man in black leather. His face was older, harder than it had been when last I saw him, but he had kept his fit soldier's physique and his hair was as black as I remembered. More importantly, he exuded the same power and confidence I had sensed on that day so many years ago when I spied on him in the soldiers' camp at Journe's Well. I thought of him then as the dark man and he still fit that description.

It was as if I stepped back into my childhood self and there I was again, crouching beside my mother on that rock, the two of us looking down on the one she said would be a great man one day. How had I not known until this moment that the dark man and the Praetor were one and the same? I felt my mother was with me even now, reaching across the barriers of time and death to impart a final secret.

On a wild whim, I opened up my senses and let the full force of all the life around me come flooding in. I was overwhelmed by the magic at first, drowning in a sea of emotions, resentments, fears, and hungers. It took me a moment to steady myself, filter out the jumbled feelings of the surrounding crowd, and focus on one man alone.

When my mind made contact with the Praetor's, the force of the meeting was like a hammer's blow. I felt his very essence more powerfully than I ever felt that of any other. For a brief instant, I knew him down to the finest nuances of his being, the deepest secrets buried in the recesses of his mind. I knew hopes and terrors even he had forgotten. Memories-that weren't mine poured through me— the taste of a wine he hadn't drank since he was a boy, the long ago excitement of pouring over maps in his father's study, the clear recollection of his mother's voice...

Lost inside the Praetor's mind, I didn't immediately notice the outward change in him. He had been speaking to a companion at his side, but his words cut off abruptly and he jerked as if stung by a wasp. He whipped his head from side to side and then something drew his gaze right to me, even lost as I was in the crowd.

When those cold eyes settled over me, I froze like a hare sighting a fox, heart thrumming against my ribcage, mouth suddenly so dry it might've been filled with dust. With a guilty start, I tried to withdraw from his mind and slip back into mine, but something in him grabbed hold of my consciousness, an unfamiliar magic stronger than any I had encountered. It refused to let me go. Realizing in a panic that if I had achieved such a complete glimpse into his memories, he could sift just as easily through mine, I struggled harder to extricate myself.

Fate intervened then. One moment I was locked in a hopeless struggle between my magic and that of the Praetor. The next, a third party stepped into the fray, plucking me loose from the Praetor's grasp and pulling me into the safety of my own self.

I was vaguely aware of being physically grabbed by the arm and dragged down from the block where I had stood. Dazed, I stumbled stupidly and someone took hold of me around the waist, another person pulling my arm over his shoulder. Together my rescuers supported and propelled me through the oblivious crowd.

CHAPTER TWELVE

A SHORT TIME LATER, I FOUND myself seated in a corner of the crowded common room of an inn. Hadrian was at one end of our narrow table, while Fleet sat opposite him, his back to the wall so no one could approach our gathering without us becoming aware of them. I was caught in the middle between my two friends, without commanding the attention of either.

I stared at the dented mug in my hands. At first, the drink served to clear my head, as Fleet promised it would, but after two rounds it was beginning to have the opposite effect, leaving me thick-headed and irritable. The noise in the common room, combined with exhaustion after my recent ordeal, awoke a dull ache in the back of my skull. Or maybe that was the effects of the drink, I thought, staring suspiciously into its murky depths.

"You aren't listening to what I say," Hadrian reprimanded me. At least, I thought it was me he was speaking to, before I realized it was Fleet he addressed.

"It was no magicker who attacked Ilan,"

Hadrian said. "If anyone other than her had been wielding the talent, I would have sensed it and I didn't. All I was aware of was her magic and that it was in some kind of trouble. I used mine to drag her back into herself, but I couldn't see what she was fighting."

Somewhere along the way, we crossed over the point where we didn't discuss magic in front of Fleet. I had been too much affected by my encounter in the street for pretense and had spilled the whole story to them both after their timely rescue. I have to give Fleet credit. Unsettling as the average person would have found it to discover himself in the presence of a magicker, the street thief absorbed the shock with typical aplomb.

"You stick to your spell casting and poofs of smoke, priest," he was saying now. "And leave me to determine when there's danger afoot and from what direction it comes. I have your mysterious magicker for you. Living on the streets has endowed me with certain instincts, and when I look at the Praetor I see menace and magic, one as clear as the other."

He was following a familiar vein but one neither of us had been able to persuade the priest to believe.

Hadrian said dryly, "How interesting that you didn't see 'menace and magic' before today."

Fleet shrugged. "I never really looked for it before. Not in him," he said. "I turn my head the other way when I see the Praetor or his friends coming down the street in their fancy carriages. There's nothing in the kingdom valuable enough to be worth the risk of slipping my hand into one of their silk purses. It'd be the chopping block for me for sure."

He chopped a hand down on the scarred tabletop for emphasis, rattling our mugs.

"Lower your voice, you idiot," Hadrian commanded, using a filthy rag at the end of the table to sop up the drops that had sloshed over the lip of his cup. "They don't execute by beheading in the province, but I've no desire to sample the more local means of justice we'll soon find tightened around our necks if you keep bellowing out secrets like they're for sale."

"The Praetor is a mage," I said quietly. "That's why you couldn't sense his kind of magic, Hadrian. It's not the Natural sort."

The bickering came to a brief halt and two heads swiveled to look at me as if they had forgotten I was there.

"You finish your drink," Hadrian ordered sharply.

Then they returned to their argument. Reluctantly, I did as I was told. No one cared for my opinion. They heard all the explanation I had to offer and decided it was between the two of them to figure out what really happened. *How did it come to this?* I asked myself a little resentfully. I was in command of the situation when we set out this morning, but since the Praetor's attack, if attack it had been, all authority had been snatched from my hands, to be wrestled back and forth between my companions.

"I brought her to get a look at the boy," Hadrian was saying. "How was I to know what would happen? I had no idea she had magic-wielding enemies."

He looked at me as if I had intentionally neglected to tell him that fact.

Tired of being chided and talked over, I shook off the lingering effects of the incident and stepped back into my usual role.

"I don't believe it was a deliberate attack," I put in firmly. "I think someone, a magicker, sensed my talent and was merely attempting to take my measure. It seems certain it was the Praetor, since I was already linked to him, but I cannot prove it to satisfaction, so make of that what you will."

"But I would have—"

I cut off Hadrian's protest. "I know. You would have been aware of his talent if it was Natural, but isn't it possible you would fail to sense Trained magic?"

Hadrian's face darkened and I knew he didn't like discussing unnatural forms of magic. He felt I took too much interest in them. But I refused to ignore what looked like the most obvious answer.

"You have your opinion," he replied. "But the truth is, we may never know who or what it was you encountered with your magic. And all of this is a far cry from what I had planned for the day. I'm afraid we've lost sight of our original purpose. To bring you to your young friend."

"It's not too late for that," I protested. "I'm feeling steadier already."

That last wasn't entirely honest, but I didn't care. I had no intention of missing my meeting with Terrac.

"The opportunity is long past," Hadrian said. "He was in the Praetor's procession and you've already missed him."

Terrac riding in the Praetor's hunting party? That raised such a string of questions I hardly knew where to begin.

Hadrian anticipated my amazement. "I thought it would be better if you saw him for yourself," he told me. "But as that chance is past, perhaps it's best I just tell you."

"The only thing I want you to tell me is why my friend is parading around with the Praetor like some kind of prince, when he should be rotting away in prison, keeping company with old bones and rats."

I felt lightheaded again but pushed the buzzing sensation to the back of my mind. Something was wrong with the picture Hadrian was painting, and I couldn't be distracted from it.

"I can't fully answer your question," Hadrian said. "All I know is what gossip the Fist lieutenant was careless enough to share. According to him, a few months ago a lad who'd been running with the outlaws of Dimmingwood was brought into Selbius. Initially imprisoned on charges of involvement with the infamous outlaw Rideon the

Red Hand, the boy might have hung for that alone, but there was the additional matter of his having nearly killed a Fist in his attempt to escape arrest."

I remembered how Terrac had stabbed a Fist when we fled the ambush at Red Rock.

Hadrian continued with, "As if the first two charges weren't bad enough, a handful of vengeful Fists stepped forward to identify the youth as one accused of recently burning down a hold house along the Selbius Road. Apparently, a number of Fists sheltered inside the house barely escaped with their lives."

Hadrian looked at me with raised brows, but I kept my expression bland. I had previously left that detail out of the tale when I recounted it to Hadrian, fearing it would make him less sympathetic to Terrac's plight.

"The Fists are known not only for their staunch loyalty to the Praetor, but also to one another," Hadrian said. "The accusations against the boy didn't sit lightly with them, and they were eager to make a quick end of the accused."

"You paint a dark picture for Terrac," I said. "If things were so against him, why is he alive and, from the sound of things, prospering?"

"Because something happened," Hadrian said. "Nobody knows what, except that the Praetor intervened in the case, suddenly and without explanation, pardoning the young outlaw for his crimes. Not only that, but he appears to have taken a personal interest in the boy, placing him under the tutelage of his arms master to be trained for future admission into the city guard. He may even advance into the ranks of the Iron Fists when he is grown, an idea that has the Praetor's guard in a sour mood indeed."

I was silent. My perception of the situation had been turned on its head so completely I hardly knew from which angle to take hold of it anymore. Such a short time ago I had been the heroic savior. I had been dashing, if a little clumsily, to the aid of the suffering captive. And now I was suddenly hit in the face with the information that Terrac was hardly languishing in captivity, in fact, that he didn't need my aid at all.

I shook my head. This should be good news. The important thing was that Terrac was out of danger. By all logic I should be pleased with the situation, since his safety was what I set out to accomplish in the first place. But the news did little to soften the knot sitting in the pit of my stomach whenever I thought of Terrac. It was no good wondering why it remained there. There was only one way to be rid of it.

"I need to see him," I told the others.

Silence descended and I looked up to find my companions regarding me incredulously.

It was Fleet who voiced the question. "Why? I understood your wanting to rescue him before, but he doesn't need saving now. What's the point of endangering yourself just for a look at him?"

Not wanting them to see I was as confused

about my reasons as they were, I could only repeat that I had to see him. I hadn't expected them to fight me on this. They had followed me easily enough before.

"Ilan," Hadrian said with a trace of sympathy. "Not only are the circumstances of this Terrac of yours perfectly comfortable, they are improved. He has the sponsorship of the very Praetor. Whatever excitement he used to enjoy, running free in Dimmingwood with you, I think you must admit it can scarcely compete with the easy life he has now. That's why you have to let him be. I know this isn't the ending you hoped for, but surely you're unselfish enough to think of Terrac's best interests."

"Unselfish?" I asked, so offended my voice quivered. "What have I been if not unselfish? Do you think I wanted to risk my life coming to this city, passing under the nose of the city guard every day, exposing myself to the Fists? Well, I didn't. And I certainly didn't want to trade Dimmingwood for some leaky, smelly river barge either. But I did that for Terrac. So forgive me if I'm not ready to call it over, not until I'm thoroughly convinced of his safety—and it will take more than the ramblings of a drunken Fist to persuade me."

Hadrian and Fleet frowned, but I could see I had succeeded in swaying them. Fleet tapped his fingers on the tabletop and looked thoughtful. "You know," he said. "I just might have an idea."

Two hours later, I was asking myself what madness had come over me to allow Fleet to take charge of anything. My desperation was no excuse. The street thief was lack-brained, I knew he was lack-brained, and yet I had followed his lead. What did that say for my own sense?

The two of us crouched behind a low stone wall, overlooking the practice yards of the Praetor's keep. My knees were buried deep in straw, the upper half of my face raised just enough to peer over the top of the wall.

Even as I complied with Fleet's precautions, I protested. "This is ridiculous. Its broad daylight and I've never been more conspicuous in my life. We'd be much less remarkable just standing in the open, gawking."

"You worry too much," Fleet said. "If anybody notices a couple extra pairs of eyes peeping over the back wall, they'll chalk it up to stable boys spying on the guardsmen at weapons practice. Anyway, I'm not about to stand out in the yard, mingling with Fists, if that's what you're suggesting. Just keep your head low and look casual, and we're all right."

"Sure," I grumbled. "We're real casual."

I returned my attention to the practice yards. "What exactly am I looking for anyway?" I asked. "You said you could get me in to see Terrac, but I've been sitting here until my knees ache and all I've seen so far are a bunch of stenched Fists and city guardsmen, wrestling and grunting like overgrown farm boys."

"Enough with the whining," he said. "What have you got to complain about, I'd like to know? You have this nice cool shade to wait in, plenty of clean fresh water over there in the trough, if you work up a thirst, and the best entertainment any girl could wish for. I'll tell you, there's more than a handful of noble young ladies who'd trade their best stockings for an eyeful of the show you're seeing. That's the province's best stock out there. Real fighting men." He dug me in the ribs, adding with a knowing grin, "Handsome devils, aren't they? I'll bet you've got your eye on the big shirtless lad over there."

Disgusted, I shook my head and fended off his bony elbow.

"Noble ladies," I snorted, when the rib digging and elbow fencing died down. "If you've ever stepped within a dozen paces of a lady, except for the time it took to lift her purse, I'll kiss a slop-sucking pig."

I missed whatever retort he came back with, because my eyes suddenly lit on a lone figure entering the yard. My stomach tightened as recognition struck, and almost without my being aware of it, a stronger emotion stirred at the back of my consciousness. It was good to see Terrac again.

It had only been a few months since we were last together, but as I studied him, I noted the little differences. He had lost the woods garb I last saw him in, traded for a new leather jerkin over cotton shirt and trousers. His clothing was simple but well made and easily marked him as one of middle station. If I saw him on the street, I would think him the servant of a merchant or nobleman. Not elegant enough for a house servant maybe, but he looked the part of a gardener or a stable hand. He had a strong, well-fed look and I thought proudly that was due to the healthy food and exercise we provided for him in Dimming. He'd been a scrawny runt when he came to us, but look at him now. He almost, but not quite, cut a pretty figure out there in the practice yard. Or maybe it only seemed that way because he had a lot of ugly Fists as a backdrop.

My satisfaction vanished when I saw the heavy blade hanging at his hip. I had seen him with a sword before on a few occasions, such as when we fought mock battles with Dradac, but this weapon looked wrong on the boy who had once wanted to be a priest. Maybe that was only because it so much resembled the kind of blade a Fist would carry. I turned my attention to his face, still dominated by the startling violet eyes that had arrested me on our first meeting all those years ago. His jaw was clenched now, as it often was when he was feeling determined or excessively stubborn, and that helped to make him look a little less ridiculous in the midst of the older men in the practice yard. Even so, he seemed to me like a fierce little terrier among wolfhounds, and I wondered what he did here.

I wasn't so distracted by the question that I failed to take in the detail that was of most interest. He showed not the slightest sign of the injury he had taken the day of his capture in Dimming. He must have been tended by a remarkable healer, because looking at him now, I could almost believe I had dreamed up that arrow between his shoulder blades.

Terrac, unaware of my concealed eyes following him across the yard, was approaching a large red-bearded man Fleet had pointed out to me earlier as Arms Master Verrik, a man who had earned himself a reputation even as far as Dimmingwood. I had heard the former Fist spoken of with grudging respect even among Rideon's band. The fact that the man was an old nemesis of the Red Hand caused me to watch the exchange between Terrac and him with interest.

I couldn't make out their words over the distance, but the conversation ended with Terrac unbuckling his sword belt and taking up the bundled lathe the other man indicated to him. The arms master took Terrac to the center of the field, where a sturdy looking combatant was found for him. I was concerned when I saw the long-legged man they set him against, a heavily muscled Fist with the look of a veteran, but my apprehension swiftly vanished as the practice commenced and I saw the larger man seemed to bear no personal malice toward the priest boy. He fought fairly, but he didn't go easy on Terrac either. Terrac gave a better account for himself than I would have expected, and even when the match ended, as it inevitably must, with the boy flat on his back, I had to admit I was left impressed by the skill and determination with which he had fought.

I marveled over the change that had come over my friend since our parting. His sword skill was improved already under the tutelage of these men, but more than that, I sensed within him a new attitude, disturbing and unfamiliar. He appeared colder and more confident. I had to dig deep to confirm that anything of the old Terrac remained inside. But it did. I smiled, relieved, as my magic closed around the tight ball of emotion shoved far back in Terrac's subconscious mind. Conscience, principle, a smidgen of condescension...

Yes, it was all still there, just smothered under the new feelings of selfishness and ambition that would have felt perfectly normal in anyone else, yet looked out of place in Terrac. I was surprised how glad I was to rediscover the traits I had once mocked my friend for. All the same, it disturbed me to see him so at home among men like the Fists. He appeared almost to belong with them, and this was a concept I had difficulty reconciling with my memories of the cowardly priest boy who used to abhor violence of any kind.

As my thoughts raced, Terrac moved on to his next match. I watched in disbelief as he downed this combatant, then helped the man to his feet. The fallen opponent said something and the two laughed like old friends.

That decided me. Rot these Fists, I didn't know what they had done to my friend, but it was obvious they had poisoned his mind. If he were left in their care much longer I probably wouldn't know him anymore. I decided if I was going to act, this was the time for it.

"Fleet," I said. "I want to get a message to him."

Fleet, seemingly having forgotten our mission, was sitting with his back to the wall, absently shuffling a deck of greasy looking cards he carried in the inner pocket of his coat.

But I had his attention now. "You're mad," he told me, turning to peek over the wall into the practice yards. "I'm not stepping into the middle of that wasp's nest so you can visit with a Fist. This right here is as close as I get."

"He's not a Fist," I said. "He's a stupid priest boy who doesn't know what he's getting himself into, and he needs my help."

"Maybe," Fleet said doubtfully. "But he's still surrounded by blades and carries one of his own, so I wouldn't be too sure he won't turn on you. If you ask me, he looks pretty comfortable with the rest of those killers. Anyway, I think the priest was right and you should just leave him be."

Seeming to consider the matter decided, he returned his attention to his cards.

I knocked them out of his hand. "Don't be such

a coward," I said. "I can't do this alone, so you have to help me. I want a chance to gauge Terrac's reaction before I meet him, which means you're the natural choice to approach him. If he saw me, he might be startled enough to give me away."

"Give *you* away?" Fleet muttered disbelievingly, plucking the cards out of the dirt, dusting them off, and pocketing them.

"Let me tell you something, my woodsy friend," he said. "I haven't avoided a thief's brand all these years to go begging for one now. This is how I operate on the streets: casual and low profile. You try keeping a low profile hanging around the Fist's practice yards, chatting it up with the Praetor's men. Or if I'm really lucky maybe I'll even bump into a city guardsman or two. Wouldn't they love to see me on their home ground?"

"Quit your pig-squealing," I said. "I'm not asking you to talk to anybody. I'll write out the message and all you'll have to do is step up there, easy as can be, and deliver it."

That caught his attention. "You can write?"

I smiled, remembering the lessons Terrac had inflicted on me at Brig's insistence.

"Give me parchment and ink and I can write the alphabet, backwards and upside down," I said.

We had no parchment, as it turned out, and no ink either. But in the end, I removed my gray coat, slit my arm with Fleet's belt knife, and dipped my fingers in the thin trickle of blood to smear out the message across the back of the coat. Fleet watched over my shoulder all the while, and I had the satisfaction of seeing him properly impressed for once. Neither our time nor my blood were as plentiful as could have been wished, so I had to keep my message short and cut out a few letters. Still, I thought Terrac would make out what I meant.

"Cemetery tonight," I read aloud to Fleet, since he couldn't read the words for himself.

What I'd actually put down may have been closer to *Cemtry tonit*, since I wasn't quite sure of the proper spelling. I hesitated over it, squeezed out a little more blood, and painted a questionable squiggle at the end of the last word that could have passed for anything the reader wanted to imagine.

When I was satisfied with my work, Fleet disappeared into the stables and emerged a short time later, leading a scrawny stable boy out by the collar. The boy couldn't have been more than six or seven years old.

"No need for me to act the messenger," Fleet said, sounding pleased with himself. "Ticks here will deliver our little gift, won't you, Ticks, my boy?"

My silent stare must have said what I thought, but I could see Fleet was determined.

He said, "The boy's just old enough to be useful, but not bright enough to ask nosy questions. Right, Ticks?"

"Right," the smudge-faced lad chimed in happily.

Protesting wouldn't have done me any good,

because Fleet was already giving the child his instructions.

"See that young fellow out there, the one that looks paler and scrawnier than the rest?" he asked. "That's our friend and we're playing a little joke... Or something of the sort."

He sounded so uncommitted to the story I doubted a drunk on sixth day would believe him, but Ticks just nodded eagerly at every other word.

"Very good, now here's what we need from you. You want to scamper out there, quick like, and put this old coat into the hands of that fellow and, without a word to anybody else, get yourself right away again. Understood? And don't run straight back here while he's watching, but take a round about way. There's a copper penny in it, if you do the job smart."

That captured the boy's attention if nothing else did and he nodded brightly. In fact, he was so eager to set on his errand that Fleet had to catch him by the collar and hold him back.

"Hold on, hold on," he said. "You've got to say something too. Tell our friend—"

Here he hesitated, looking expectantly at me.

"Just tell him his friends from Dimmingwood are worried," I said.

Fleet turned to the boy. "You hear what she says, uh, what's your name again? Flea? Tick? Right, right, that's fine. Now off you go. Remember 'worried forest friends.' Not one word more and not one less or I'll keep your copper and tear off your ears. Got that?"

The boy nodded, his expression equal parts fear and greed, and clambered over the wall as soon as he was released. I watched as he scampered across the yard, stopping once or twice to examine a bug on the ground or to take a rock out of his shoe.

"He's going to ruin it," I said.

"Probably," Fleet agreed.

I knew the exact moment my cryptic message was reported. I couldn't hear over this distance, of course, but I saw Terrac start as the boy spoke to him. Then he twisted around as if expecting to find me only a few steps away. I thought he would never turn his attention to the delivered garment. It was a relief when he finally looked down at the bloody words scrawled there. If he appeared momentarily confused, he recovered quickly and rolled up the coat, stuffing it under one arm and glancing around, as if to be sure no one had been reading over his shoulder. When he turned to question the small messenger, our boy had already disappeared.

I leaned back, satisfied. Provided Terrac did nothing stupid, and considering his history, I didn't deem that entirely a given, we would escape tonight.

CHAPTER THIRTEEN

THE WATER CEMETERY WAS AN eerier spot than I remembered. What possessed me to name this our meeting place? It hadn't been so bad when I first arrived, passing through the gardens to enter the lonely graveyard at twilight. Then at least there had been more than moonlight to see by and the comfort of occasional bursts of laughter and conversation filtering over the walls from strolling citizens in the gardens beyond. But that had been hours ago.

The sun was down now and a grey mist rose from the waters. A cold dampness had long ago worked its way into my bones as I waited in the stillness behind the shadow of a tall, potted tree and I shivered, fuming at myself for not being more specific in my message. 'Tonight' could mean anytime between now and sunrise, and I had no desire to wait that long in this gloomy place. A chill draft crept over the high wall at my back, stirring the fronds of the surrounding plants and sending another shiver through me as its fingers caressed my spine. I turned up the collar of the new coat Fleet had procured for me and, shifting my weight so the foot I crouched on could get a little blood back into it, schooled myself to patience.

Gazing over the dark waters before me, I tried to convince myself the tiny ripples disturbing the moon's reflection were only fish snatching at insects on the surface. The rustling noises occasionally coming from the surrounding greenery were surely just small animals creeping into the cemetery to nibble at the plants. Even so, the goose pimples standing out on my flesh weren't due entirely to the cold. Something nudged my shoulder softly and I whirled around, but it was only the spindly branch of another potted tree.

A flash of movement on one of the distant walkways spanning the cemetery waters caught my eye. The moon was behind a cloud, but even in the shadows, I recognized Terrac crossing the walk. He appeared to hesitate, stopping halfway across the bridge to peer uncertainly into the shadows. My heart picked up pace at the sight of him, although it was only a matter of hours since I'd watched him at sword practice. I didn't try to puzzle out the unexpected rush of emotion I experienced as I felt his familiar presence wash over me. This was a time for action, not contemplation.

I waited just long enough to be sure he was unaccompanied and, when my searching senses confirmed we were alone, abandoned my hiding place. I saw him start as I left the shadows and crossed into the open and, even as I stepped onto the bridge, Fleet's final words of warning rang in my ears. The street thief hadn't wanted me to come alone, had tried to dissuade me from coming at all. "There was something untrustworthy about this Terrac," Fleet said. I tried to shake away the doubts, but a niggling voice kept reminding me how easily I could be walking into a Fists' trap.

We met at the center of the span. I hadn't exactly been expecting a teary embrace, but a simple "good to see you" would have been nice. Instead, we paused with a short distance still between us, eyeing one another warily. The night breeze whipped back Terrac's long coat, affording a glimpse of the Fist-style blade buckled at his hip.

My eyes flickered toward it for only a moment before returning to the face of my childhood friend. Viewing him up close, I was vaguely alarmed to realize I could almost have been looking at a stranger. More subtle changes had taken place than those I noticed back at the Fists' practice yard. He was taller and broader, but I could deal with that. I'd known the day would eventually come when I would have to tilt my head to look up at him. What I hadn't been prepared for was the way the past few months had added years to his face. The boyish roundness had melted from his features, leaving his cheekbones and stubborn jaw more prominent than ever. A jaw that, if my eyes weren't deceiving me, now sported the faintest shadow of whiskers.

If this wasn't shock enough, there was something unfamiliar in his gaze. I was reminded suddenly that I had dressed uncharacteristically in a city woman's billowy skirts and wore my hair loose, instead of in its usual braid down my back. No wonder he scarcely recognized me. But still he knew me. There was a glint in his eyes that said so, just as I couldn't mistake him, even with a little maturity added to his face and the clothes of a city man on his back.

I watched in dismay as his initial expression was replaced by one of distrust. I'd known him long enough to guess what he was thinking.

"I didn't come here to make trouble for you, Terrac," I said.

From the way he started it was clear he'd forgotten how easily I used to guess his feelings, but he recovered quickly. "Why then?" he asked. "You've seen I do well for myself now. Why should you suddenly show up, if not to gain anything? I suppose Rideon sent you to discover what I've told the Fists, maybe even to silence me. If so, you can tell your great captain he has nothing to fear. I haven't compromised any of his secrets, not because I was unwilling to, but because I didn't know anything... A small favor and the last he'll be getting from me. Tell him so."

My jaw could have scraped the cobbles. And not only because he'd never had the nerve to speak to me like that back in Dimming, but because his speech made it clear he now considered me the enemy. No, worse than that, he thought I was the lowly *messenger* of the enemy.

But I kept my feelings under control. "I don't know what you're babbling about, Terrac, but Rideon didn't send me and would be furious if he knew I was here," I said.

"So, what then? Am I supposed to believe you came merely for the sake of friendship?" he asked.

"Well, isn't that what we are? Friends?" I asked. "I don't think anybody who considered themselves less than a friend would follow you all the way to Selbius and put themselves through the risks I have to help you escape."

He looked confused. "Escape? Escape from what?"

"From the Fists, of course," I said. "You can't tell me you *want* to be their prisoner? I've come to take you home."

His laughter frightened the birds in the treetops overhead, and they scattered into the night sky. "Home?" he repeated. "You cannot be serious. You really think Dimmingwood was ever home to me?"

Despite myself, I was nettled by his ingratitude. "I fail to see what amuses you," I said. "I've sacrificed a lot to save your worthless hide. But I'm not about to waste one more day in this city, so I suggest you stop yammering and we get busy putting this place behind us. I hope you brought everything you plan on taking with you, because I'm not going back to the Praetor's keep for anything."

He ignored the question. "So let me get this straight. I finally break free of the band of villainous brigands who've been holding me prisoner for over two years, make it to a place of safety where I can return to my interrupted life, and now here comes one of the outlaws, offering to drag me back to their miserable forest?"

I masked my hurt. "That's about the size of it," I said. "Shall we get started?"

He snorted. "Can you really imagine I'm eager to go running back to the place where I spent the worst days of my life? I was little more than an unpaid servant to your disgusting company of criminals, whereas I have a comfortable place here."

"Here?" I asked blankly. "Here meaning the Praetor's household?"

When he looked surprised, I added, "Yes, I know all about that because I've asked around about you. I've heard how you crawled into the Praetor's employ, and I've seen you train side by side with his Fists. Tell me, what are you playing at? You talk of reclaiming an interrupted life, but the last I remember, you were headed for the priesthood. How can you have changed so much?"

If the sense of betrayal I felt showed in my words, it didn't move him as it once would have. Terrac only narrowed his eyes. "My private plans are my own concern," he said. "You'd best look to yours, outlaw."

Stunned, I lashed out with the first thing that came to mind. "The Terrac I remember wouldn't have turned his back on old friends to join with their enemies."

That appeared to shame him a little, and an

uncertain expression flitted across his features. For just a moment, I felt I was looking at the old Terrac.

"Did you truly come to save me?" he asked quietly.

"I did. But it grows clear my efforts aren't wanted. Since it turns out you're enjoying the company of your captors, I suppose I'll leave you to them."

"I told you; I'm no prisoner," he said. "As soon as it was discovered I was an honest man caught up in bad circumstances, I was released. The Praetor himself spoke for me."

"So I've heard," I said.

"I was grateful, of course, for his generosity in giving me a place in his house," Tearrac continued.

"Generosity?" I said. "Boast of the Praetor's generosity to the people he's murdered over the years for opposing him." It didn't seem the wisest time to bring up the cleansings instigated by the Praetor so long ago to destroy all the magickers in the province. Neither was I ready to reveal that my parents had been among his victims. Instead, I said, "What about those who've been starved and forced out of their homes by the Praetor's taxes?"

Terrac scowled. "Say what you like, but he's not a cruel man. If you've had a dark view of him, maybe it's because you've been looking on from the opposite side of the law."

His expression turned thoughtful, as he added, "He's a hard sort, I'll admit, but far from evil. He spared my life, after all."

"If the Praetor goes out of his way to save anybody, it's because he has a use for them," I warned.

"And you know him so well you can say that with authority," Terrac retorted, but there was little bite to his response. His eyes had taken on a distant look, as if recalling something he didn't especially like.

"My memories of those days in prison are shadowed in confusion," he said. "No matter when I awoke, it always seemed to be night. There was flickering torchlight, terrible smells, screams from out of the darkness... I had no way of marking the time, but I think I spent most of it in a feverish sleep. During rare moments of clarity I was aware of searing pain. I believe the wound from the arrow was infected, because the feeling was akin to what I suffered when Illsman stabbed me in the side. You remember? On the day we met?"

I did.

He continued. "There's one memory that stands out. I once awoke to find myself being rolled over, the movement causing such pain I couldn't help screaming. I heard someone saying, 'Easy, you fools, don't damage the boy!' My blood-encrusted bandages were removed with surprising care—I have no memory of how they came to be there in the first place or of the arrow being removed. Suddenly, cool hands touched my injury and then that harsh voice again, muttering strange, low words I couldn't recognize. I'd been in pain already, but now it was rolling over me in waves. Then, just as I was expecting to die, *wanting* to die, the agony vanished as quickly as it had come and with it, all traces of my injury."

Terrac's voice was low and in the glow of the moonlight I could see the sheen of sweat standing out on his forehead.

I understood it wasn't the memory of the pain that was disturbing him.

"You were healed by magic," I said.

He shifted uneasily. "Maybe."

There was no doubt in my mind. Healing through touch could be accomplished in no other way. More than that, the chanting Terrac had heard indicated the magic was the Trained work of a mage and not that of a Natural. My heart quickened as I thought of my earlier encounter on the street with a mysterious mage. From my experience and from what Terrac described, I was more certain than ever the mage was the Praetor. But that opened up a confusing array of questions.

I asked cautiously, "Do you know who this healer was? Did you get a look at him?"

"No, I sank into a long sleep after the healing," he said. "I never got a look at the man's face or had a chance to thank him."

I had always been able to tell when Terrac was lying, and he was lying now. But before I could ask whose secret he was protecting and why, we were interrupted by the distant clang of the bell in the city watchtower, striking the hour. Both of us flinched and Terrac appeared to come back to himself.

"I should be going. I have early weapons practice tomorrow," he said. "Besides, the city guard patrols these grounds and I don't think it would be good for either of us..."

I smiled thinly. "Of course. You can't afford to be found in company like mine now that you've got such a bright future ahead of you."

"It isn't me who's in danger here. I'll never know what possessed you to take such risks, but if you're wise you'll get out of Selbius while you can. Go back to Dimmingwood, where you'll be safe."

I eyed him. "I detect a note of urgency in your warning. Why such haste? Am I in danger of betrayal?"

He looked everywhere but at me. "I won't report your contact with me this time," he mumbled. "But I'll be honor-bound to in the future. Now that the Praetor is my master, well... Plainly spoken, it would be best if we didn't meet again."

"I see." I wasn't sure who I was angriest with, him for his betrayal or myself for feeling disappointment. What had I expected from him anyway? He had grown up, cast aside his old ideas about honor, and was learning to protect himself first and forget everyone else. Wasn't that something I'd struggled to teach him for years? Evidently his new master, the Praetor, had been able to accomplish the lesson more quickly.

I had no opportunity to put these thoughts into words because Terrac was already backing away, his boots scraping over the stone walk. I sensed his eagerness to end this uncomfortable interview and realized suddenly that I shared it.

"Good-bye then, priest boy," I said quietly. But he was already so far away I couldn't be sure he heard.

NOT AN ENDING, BUT
A RESTING PLACE

I T ISN'T UNTIL NOW, AS I stand on the deck of
the river barge, battered by the wind and the
spray of the storm, and look toward the dark,
distant walls of Selbius, that I realize what disturbs
me most about my meeting with Terrac. He was
wearing my brooch, the gift from my mother that
had been supposed, at one time, to save me. I
know how he came by it, remember him pocketing
it shortly before the ambush at Red Rock. But why
does he wear it now and what, if any, part does it
play in his newly found good fortune?

Lightning splits the sky and a clap of thunder
deafens me, but neither is what sends me scurrying
for the dry shelter of Seephinia's hut. Something
in there calls to me, a haunting voice sighing
through my mind, whispering plans for the future.
It belongs to the bow.

ABOUT THE AUTHOR

C. Greenwood is the fantasy pen name of author Dara England, who lives in Oklahoma with her husband, two young children, and a Yorkshire terrier. To receive updates on future books, visit www.DaraEnglandAuthor.com and sign up for her monthly newsletter.

WRITING AS C. GREENWOOD

Legends of Dimmingwood Series

Magic of Thieves ~ Book I
Betrayal of Thieves ~ Book II
Circle of Thieves ~ Book III
Redemption of Thieves ~ Book IV

Other Titles

Dreamer's Journey

WRITING AS DARA ENGLAND

The Accomplished Mysteries

Accomplished in Murder ~ Book One
Accomplished in Detection ~ Book Two
Accomplished in Blood ~ Book Three

The American Heiress Mysteries

Death on Dartmoor ~ Book One
Murder in Mayfair ~ Book Two

Other Titles

Beastly Beautiful
Love By The Book
The Magic Touch
*Eternal Strife (The Mammoth
Book of Irish Romance)*

Made in the USA
San Bernardino, CA
09 April 2014